MURDER FOR ART'S SAKE

Books by Frances and Richard Lockridge

Cats

THE CAT WHO RODE COWS
THE NAMELESS CAT
THE PROUD CAT
CATS AND PEOPLE
THE LUCKY CAT

Mr. and Mrs. North

MURDER BY THE BOOK
MURDER HAS ITS POINTS
THE JUDGE IS REVERSED
MURDER IS SUGGESTED
THE LONG SKELETON
VOYAGE INTO VIOLENCE
DEATH OF AN ANGEL
A KEY TO DEATH
DEATH HAS A SMALL VOICE
CURTAIN FOR A JESTER
DEAD AS A DINOSAUR
MURDER COMES FIRST
MURDER IN A HURRY
MURDER IS SERVED
UNTIDY MURDER
DEATH OF A TALL MAN
MURDER WITHIN MURDER
PAYOFF FOR THE BANKER
KILLING THE GOOSE
DEATH TAKES A BOW
HANGED FOR A SHEEP
DEATH ON THE AISLE
MURDER OUT OF TURN
A PINCH OF POISON
THE NORTHS MEET MURDER
MR. AND MRS. NORTH
THE DISHONEST MURDERER

Captain Heimrich

THE DISTANT CLUE
FIRST COME, FIRST KILL
—WITH ONE STONE
SHOW RED FOR DANGER
ACCENT ON MURDER
PRACTISE TO DECEIVE
LET DEAD ENOUGH ALONE
BURNT OFFERING
DEATH AND THE GENTLE BULL
STAND UP AND DIE
DEATH BY ASSOCIATION
A CLIENT IS CANCELED
FOGGY, FOGGY DEATH
SPIN YOUR WEB, LADY!
I WANT TO GO HOME
THINK OF DEATH

Mystery Adventures

THE DEVIOUS ONES
QUEST OF THE BOGEYMAN
NIGHT OF SHADOWS
THE TICKING CLOCK
AND LEFT FOR DEAD
THE DRILL IS DEATH
THE GOLDEN MAN
MURDER AND BLUEBERRY PIE
THE INNOCENT HOUSE
CATCH AS CATCH CAN
THE TANGLED CORD
THE FACELESS ADVERSARY

Mysteries by Richard Lockridge

MURDER FOR ART'S SAKE
MURDER ROUNDABOUT
SQUIRE OF DEATH
MURDER CAN'T WAIT

Novels by Richard Lockridge

A MATTER OF TASTE
THE EMPTY DAY
ENCOUNTER IN KEY WEST

Murder For Art's Sake

BY RICHARD LOCKRIDGE

J. B. LIPPINCOTT COMPANY
Philadelphia *New York*

FIRST EDITION

PRINTED IN THE UNITED STATES OF AMERICA

LIBRARY OF CONGRESS CATALOG CARD NUMBER 67–13301

For Hildy

MURDER FOR ART'S SAKE

I

SHE PAID THE cabdriver. She stood on the sidewalk and watched the cab roll slowly down the street to the next corner. It hesitated there and then made a right turn. That was the way she had told the driver would be the simplest out of the jigsaw of streets she had guided him into. After the cab was out of sight she stood for some seconds in front of the tottering old building and knew she was postponing, and that it was useless to postpone.

The three flights of stairs would not grow less steep because of her delay. The treads would remain as narrow. She took a deep breath in preparation and went into the building. She hesitated again at the foot of the first flight, but this time only for a moment. She climbed it, holding onto the handrail and feeling the same sense of insecurity she always felt. The stairs canted away from the wall and she thought, as she had so often thought, that one day the whole building would tumble down. She had said that often enough, and had been snorted at for saying it.

She went along the corridor of the second floor to the foot of the next flight. Her heels clattered on the worn bare boards of the corridor. She climbed again, and at the top of the flight she paused to catch her breath, holding to the handrail.

She walked the third-floor corridor and climbed the final flight and stood in front of the familiar door. She groped the key out of her handbag and put it in the keyhole and tried to turn it to the right.

It would not turn.

For an instant, then, she thought that he might have had the lock changed. It didn't seem likely. Then she realized that she had, once more, made a mistake. If the key was pushed too far into the keyhole, even by the smallest fraction of an inch too far, it would not turn. She eased it out that smallest fraction of an inch, and turned it and the lock clicked. She pushed the door open and, as she stepped into the big cluttered room, she called, "Shack? You here, Shack?"

She called loudly and was not answered. She called again, the door still open behind her, and then, leaving the door partly open, went on into the room—into the unpartitioned area which was the whole of the fourth floor of the loft building. She went only a little way and stopped, and put both hands up to her mouth for an instant.

He had bled a good deal there on the floor in front of the small easel. The blood had spread out from his body. He lay face down and there was a hole in the back of his head, behind the right ear. The revolver was on the floor near his outstretched right hand.

Her screams slashed through the emptiness of the great room. Now she had started to scream she could not stop. She turned away and went back toward the door, her steps uncertain, almost stumbling. She heard the screaming continue, but it was as if somebody else were screaming.

She pulled the door open and held to the knob and then there were words in the scream. "Help!" she cried. "Help!"

She groped her way to the head of the stairs and screamed down them.

For a moment she thought that she still was not heard. She began to go down the steps. But then, from two floors below, she heard a door slam open and the banging of feet on the stairs.

Still holding to the stair rail she sank down to sit on the top step.

The man who ran along the corridor below and then up the stairs toward her was thick-set. He wore a white shirt open at the neck. When he was halfway up the staircase toward her he stopped and said, "What's the matter, lady?" He spoke loudly. He almost shouted the words.

She gestured behind her with her free hand and then, slowly, pulled herself to her feet.

"Mr. Jones," she said. "In there." Again she gestured toward the open door of the fourth-floor loft. "He's—he's *dead!* He's ——" Her voice broke off, and she stood against the wall to let the thick-set man go past her. Then she spoke again, her voice low, shaking, but audible. "He's killed himself," she said. "Shack's shot himself."

Then, leaning against the wall, she began to sob.

II

Detective Lieutenant Nathan Shapiro looked around the enormous room and realized that he was entirely beyond his depth. This did not surprise him; he was accustomed to his inadequacy and only astonished that it was not universally recognized. Captain William Weigand, in command of Homicide, South, should have been the first, after Shapiro himself, to realize his subordinate's limitations.

"Looks like suicide, Nate," Weigand said that June afternoon. "Precinct's satisfied. M.E.'s man isn't. Angle of entry apparently. So it comes through 'suspicious death.' You can have Tony Cook."

Detective (1st Grade) Anthony Cook had some difficulty in finding Little Great Smith Street, and poked the police car into numerous wrong turnings before he did. Cook had recently been transferred from a precinct squad in the Bronx, for reasons which baffled him. He knew every byway of the Bronx precinct. *Little* Great Smith Street, indeed! The whole of Greenwich Village, for that matter. A region in which there was an intersection of West Fourth and West Twelfth streets, by all that was holy!

Shapiro sighed his sympathy and thought wistfully of Brooklyn, where he had first walked a beat. And where, for his money, he should still be walking one. The Police Department of the City of New York was clearly out of its collective mind. *Lieutenant* Nathan Shapiro, by all that was holy.

"Might try the next left," he said to Detective Cook, and Cook said, "You're the boss," and tried it. He had to nudge the curb of a narrow street so that the mortuary van could inch past. The driver of the van jerked a directing thumb, pointing behind him. Beyond a jog, police cars clogged the street, which had jogged itself a change of name from "Albert" to "Little Great Smith."

The lab truck had had to park on the sidewalk. Cook edged the squad car in behind it.

The loft building the cars clustered in front of listed considerably to what Shapiro took to be the west. But the three flights of stairs they climbed listed to what Shapiro took to be the east. They also creaked. Doors of two of the lofts they climbed past had lettering on them: IMPERIAL NOVELTIES, INC. That was the first floor. PERMA-SNAPS. That was the second. The third floor of the loft building–a building which should, Lieutenant Shapiro morosely thought, have been condemned twenty years ago–was unoccupied.

The door of the fourth-floor loft was half open. A sheet of paper was tacked to it, and on the paper, climbing up it, lettered in black, was the single word "Shack." At least, the word looked rather like "Shack." Printed, Shapiro thought, by a child. Probably a somewhat backward child. He pushed the door farther open.

The room was enormous; the room was the whole floor. A skylight slanted over half of it. No sun shone through the skylight. Of course–north light. The room was unexpectedly cool. Because sunlight did not reach into it? No. The unpartitioned room was air-conditioned. Shapiro had had a room air conditioner installed in his Brooklyn apartment and it had been expensive as hell. What it must have cost to air-condition this space–fifty feet wide by a hundred deep, at a guess–baffled the easily baffled mind of Nathan Shapiro. More, he thought, than the whole of the building was worth. In the approximate center of the loft a single wooden column held the ceiling up. For the moment, Shapiro thought. The supporting column listed, like everything else.

There were a good many men in the room and they were doing familiar things. One man held a sketch pad and penciled rapidly on it–he was making a plan of the room. Two men were dusting for fingerprints, dusting a wooden chair and a wooden table deep in the room, and the sills of windows which, at the far end, let in a little of the afternoon's sunlight. Precinct and police lab were doing their job, whether or not it was a job worth doing.

Lieutenant Myron Jacobs, of the precinct detective squad, stood at one side of the room, under the skylight, and looked thoughtfully at the floor.

Shapiro walked over to him and Jacobs quit regarding the floor and regarded Nathan Shapiro; looked up and down a long thin man with a long sad face and sad brown eyes. He said, "So you got it, did you, Nate?" and Shapiro said it looked like it, his voice as sad as his face. He looked again around the room and sighed. He looked down at the floor, and at the chalked outline marking what once had been a man. There was a good deal of blood on the floor within the outline and beyond it. The blood had seeped into the cracks between the floor boards and congealed there.

"Behind the right ear," Jacobs said. "Gun on the floor where it would have been. Thirty-two revolver."

"*Behind* the right ear?"

"You and Doc Simpson," Jacobs said. "Could have managed it. Used his thumb on the trigger. Didn't want to see what he was doing to himself. Happens that way. You know that, Nate."

"Contact?"

"You and the doc. So he didn't want to feel it against his head. Suicides do funny things. You know that, Nate. Take a man decides to cut his throat. Half the time he makes a couple of false starts before he gets his nerve up."

"The gun?"

"All right. Smudges. What we usually get off a hand gun. Ballistics has taken it along. You're in late on it, Nate."

Nathan Shapiro said, "Yeah," and looked again around the room. It was cluttered with canvases with paint on them. They were stacked against the walls haphazardly. They were in grooved racks. They were on easels scattered around the enormous room. The easel nearest the chalked outline which showed where a man had fallen and where he had died had a sheet of drawing paper tacked to it, and there were black marks on the paper's whiteness. Vaguely, distortedly, the marks seemed to add up to the sketch of a woman. A very peculiar looking woman, certainly. All height; no width. Perhaps not a woman at all; perhaps a plucked ostrich. Shapiro shook his head with no hope that shaking would clear it. It was entirely beyond him and he had every expectation that it would remain there.

He tried, with no special success, to avoid looking at the paintings which were in sight. Looking at them would, he realized, only make bad matters worse. He had never realized there were so many possible colors or that they could be so bewilderingly spread on canvas.

"Supposed to be paintings," Jacobs said. "Make any sense to you, Nate?"

"No."

"School my kid goes to," Jacobs said, "they have what they call 'Art.' Give the kids paints and paper and tell them to go at it. Listen, Nate, Junior's only six. They let him bring home one of his pictures and you could tell right away it was a picture of a cow. God knows where he ever saw a cow, but you could tell it was a cow."

"Central Park Zoo," Shapiro said. "They've got a cow there, Jake."

He looked again at the easel in front of which, at a guess, Shackleford Jones had been standing when he decided to shoot himself. The longer he looked at it, the more easily Nathan Shapiro could understand what had driven Jones to his irrevocable decision. My God, Jones had probably thought, I did *that*. And went and got a gun.

"His revolver?" Shapiro asked.

The check on that wasn't completed. Jones had had a pistol permit, and Records would come up with the serial number and match it with the gun which had been on the floor. And the pathologist would get the bullet out of what had been a painter's brain and, if it was not too battered by the bone it had crushed, Ballistics would use a comparison microscope. But it was a hundred to one Shackleford Jones had used his own gun to fire a bullet into his own head. A thousand to one, Lieutenant Myron Jacobs figured it.

"Some of these young docs," Jacobs said.

Shapiro did not reply to that. Shooting one's self in the back of the head was, after all, doing it the hard way. Holding a revolver at some distance from the head would be doing it the chancy way. But with a man who thus used paint on canvas, sketched on white paper, almost any other idiosyncrasy was possible. Even to be expected.

"We're about finished," Jacobs said, and watched the fingerprint men walk the long length of the room. "Apparently nobody ever dusted the damn place," one of them said, in passing. "Prints all over everywhere." "You boys have fun," Jacobs said, and turned back to Nathan Shapiro.

"You, too, if you figure you've got to push it around," he said. "You and your side-kick. New in Homicide, isn't he?"

"Name of Cook," Shapiro said. "Transferred from the Bronx. Broke the Burnside kill. More or less by himself, apparently. Yes, we'll look around a bit more. Not that we'll turn up anything. He live here?"

Shackleford Jones had not been supposed to live in the studio loft. There are laws governing such matters. For some years painters had been protesting, singly and in groups, the enforcement of those laws. They had also been circumventing the laws.

"No gear," Jacobs said. "There's a cot back there behind things"—he pointed back there behind things. "Nothing to prove Jones used it. What this dealer of his says, he's got a place over on East Eighth Street. It's being checked out."

Nathan Shapiro mentally noted an address on East Eighth Street. It would be a place to go to duplicate effort. It was a nuisance to come in four hours late. Late, a Homicide man was supposed to find things others had missed. Such a supposition in relation to Shapiro was, he knew, absurd. Because a man has been lucky once or twice and is good with a gun—that much Nathan Shapiro would grant himself—people get confused ideas.

"I'll poke around a while," Shapiro told Lieutenant Myron Jacobs. "How'd he get a pistol permit?"

Jacobs had no idea. Probably Jones had had an in somewhere. Could be he had persuaded somebody that the contents of the studio had monetary value. Jacobs looked around the room.

"Jeeze!" he said. "Nothing more to do here I can see. You'll lock it up when you're ready? Snap lock."

Shapiro gloomily thought that he was ready then. All that mattered was already in hands more capable than his. He said, "O.K., Jake. We won't be long."

He went down one side of the long loft and looked at pictures, and Detective Anthony Cook went down the other.

One canvas Shapiro stopped in front of in bewilderment had two horizontal black lines parallel on it. That was all there was on it. Looked like a section of railroad track, as much as it looked like anything. But another, this one on an easel, was a tangle of shapes, done in bright colors. The shapes had, so far as Shapiro could see, no coherence and no meaning. But Shapiro stood in front of the easel for several minutes because somehow there was a challenge in what he looked at–an inexplicable excitement in what he looked at.

In the lower right-hand corner of the canvas, which was large, the word "Shack" had been lettered. The lettering was as primitive as it was on the door. The painter's signature, presumably. Did the fact he had signed it mean that he had thought it finished? Nathan Shapiro shook his head and sighed and turned to look at the outermost of several canvases stacked against the wall.

Here was another tangle of shapes and colors, but this time it vaguely suggested something to the sad-faced man. He stood and puzzled his mind with it and, unexpectedly, words came into his mind. "Wreck on the Jersey Turnpike," the words were. But there was nothing in what he saw to picture a pile-up of varicolored trailer trucks. It merely felt like that. He tilted it toward him and looked at the painting behind it. This one was framed and there was a typed label on the bottom of the frame. "#37. Still Life." That was what was on the label. And after the words "Still Life" there were figures. The figures were "4,500." A price? If so, presumably one cypher had accidentally been added. And a comma used instead of an intended period.

This painting was perhaps of a vase of flowers, but, if so, a vase listing to an impossible degree. And beside it–surely not an egg? A flower vase which had laid an egg? A green egg with white spots on it?

There was, Shapiro realized, no point whatever in going on with this. It became increasingly more probable that Precinct was right; that a man named Shackleford Jones who had hoped to be a painter, and had the money to buy canvases and paints, had looked around his barn of a studio and had seen what had come of his hopes and had, understandably, shot himself in the back of the head.

Shapiro looked around the room and for a moment the room seemed almost vocal with shape and color. For that instant he felt that he could almost understand what the room was saying. Which was absurd.

If the paintings in the room were speaking, trying above the uproar of their own colors to explain themselves, they spoke now only to Lieutenant Nathan Shapiro and Detective (1st Grade) Anthony Cook. The rest of the policemen had gone about more reasonable activities. It was high time, Shapiro thought, that he and Cook followed a good example.

Cook was standing in the most distant corner of the room, near the narrow windows. One of them had an air-conditioning unit in it. There was a fire escape beyond the other. Cook was half hidden by an easel. He was holding a sheet of paper out in front of him and looking at it. When he realized that Shapiro was looking at him, he held the drawing sheet in one hand and beckoned with the other. Shapiro walked the length of the talkative room and looked at what Cook held out for him to see.

What he saw surprised him. It was a sketch, in black and white only, of what was, recognizably, a woman—a naked woman. No woman had, Shapiro thought, ever looked quite like the woman portrayed in black charcoal on white paper. There was distortion in the drawing but there was some strange meaning in the distortion.

"Looks like she's flying," Cook said. "Damnedest thing, isn't it?"

It was the damnedest thing. It was inconceivable that the man who had painted "Wreck on the Jersey Turnpike" had made this sketch. But in the lower right-hand corner there was a signature and the signed name was "Shack." It was entirely the damnedest thing.

What it came to, Shapiro thought, was that the man had been able to draw—draw with skill and imagination, so that what he sketched became more than, yet without essentially abandoning, what was real. And Nathan Shapiro, to his entire surprise, wished that he could take this sketch home to his Brooklyn apartment and hang it on a wall. Rose would not approve of the woman's being naked, rather explicitly naked. But she would, as now he did, want to keep on looking at it.

"The rest of it I don't get," Cook said. "A lot of crazy junk, for my money. But this ——"

He stopped and both men turned and faced up the long room. A key scraped in the lock and the lock clicked. The door opened, and there was no hesitancy in its opening. Whoever had used a key to open the way into Shackleford Jones's studio did not expect to find anybody in it.

A woman came in and her movements, too, were without hesitancy. She did not look around the room; obviously did not see the men who, half hidden by easels, stood at the end of it. They stood very quietly.

The woman was tall and very thin. She wore black slacks tight on long legs and a black jumper, its turtleneck almost to her chin. She had black hair which drifted to her shoulders. She was, Shapiro guessed, over six feet tall. She was, he guessed, somewhere in her twenties. When she walked into the room her long legs took long strides.

She walked directly to the easel which had a chalked outline in front of it. She did not seem surprised to see an outline chalked there and if she saw the blood on the floor, and in the cracks of the floor, she paid no attention to it.

The drawing paper with the sketch on it of, perhaps, a woman who was all height and no width, had been thumbtacked to a board fitted into the easel's frame. The tall, black-clad woman began to loosen the thumbtacks.

Shapiro moved then, his shoes making a harsh sound on the

gritty floor. The woman turned, her right hand still holding at a thumbtack. Shapiro said, "Looking for something, miss?"

She turned away abruptly, as if about to walk toward the door, but then stopped herself and turned back to face the two men who walked toward her.

"It's mine, mister," she said. "He told me it was mine. Anyway, it's *me*."

The drawing sagged down from the easel board, only one tack holding it. Suddenly, Shapiro remembered it very clearly. In that moment he realized too, why, when the tall young woman walked with long strides into the room, he had thought there was something vaguely familiar about her. She had posed for the sketch. Presumably, and most understandably, she had come to tear it up.

"Who are you, anyway?" the tall girl said. She had, unexpectedly, a low-pitched voice.

"Police," Shapiro said. "You posed for the drawing, miss?"

"Of course," she said. "It's me. And Shack said —" She did not say what Shack had said. Instead, she said, "He owed me for the posing time. So it's mine, isn't it?"

Which was somewhat bewildering. She implied, Shapiro thought, some correlation between money owed and the plucked ostrich sketch. Which was absurd. If she wanted to destroy it, keep it out of any possible circulation, that would have been entirely reasonable. Shapiro tried to keep his bewilderment from showing in his voice.

"No," he said. "I don't know whose it will turn out to be, now that Mr. Jones is dead. You knew he was dead when you came in, didn't you?"

"Of course," she said. "Everybody knows. It was on the radio or something."

That, Shapiro thought, would be surprising, if true. Radio bulletins are selective. That an incomprehensible painter had killed himself in a loft building in the West Village would hardly seem to editors an item of importance. Probably the girl was lying; perhaps she had another way of knowing that the man who signed himself "Shack" was dead. Which would be interesting.

Her name was Rachel Farmer, if it was any of their business. She was told that it was. She had an apartment in Gay Street, if that mattered to anybody. She was a model. She posed for artists mostly. Sometimes for photographers. She was abrupt in her answers. Shapiro thought she was trying to show contempt for the triviality of the questions. She's wary, Nathan Shapiro thought, and wondered why. She did not know why they asked her these things and, No, she wouldn't sit down, because she wasn't tired and, anyway, she had an appointment. And what everybody said, Shack had killed himself, hadn't he?

"It looks that way, Miss Farmer," Shapiro said.

Then?

"We're trying to make sure that that was the way it was," Shapiro told her. "Part of the job they give us to do. How's it happen you have a key, Miss Farmer?"

"Lots of people have, mister," she said. "Shack gave lots of people keys. So that if he was working he wouldn't have to go to the door and let people in. Unless there was a sign on the door."

"Sign?"

"If he didn't want to be bothered he wrote, 'Go away' on a sheet of drawing paper and tacked it on the outside of the door."

"When were you last here, Miss Farmer? To pose for him?"

"Day before yesterday."

According to the Medical Examiner's report, Shackleford Jones had been dead between twenty and twenty-four hours when Myra Dedek had walked into the studio at about ten o'clock that Thursday morning and seen his body and begun to scream. She must have screamed loudly, because they had heard her in the loft two floors below. She must have screamed urgently, because the owner of "Perma-Snaps" had gone running up the stairs. Benjamin Negly, the owner of "Perma-Snaps" was, and he had called the police. The call had come through at 10:08 that morning.

"Not yesterday?" Shapiro asked Rachel Farmer.

"Day before," she said. "That was–what's today?"

"Thursday."

"Tuesday. At three in the afternoon. I was right on time and I stood there–" she gestured imprecisely to one side of where she stood–"for two hours. And if you moved while he was working he yelled at you. And then he said he didn't have any money and would pay me next time. He said that lots of times."

"He did pay in the end?"

"You're damn right he did," she said. "You think I pose two hours for the fun of it?"

She's being very tough, Shapiro thought. Tougher than she needs to be. But I'm no good at summing people up, at finding out what makes them tick. And I don't know anything about people like this girl–models and painters and people like that. Put me back on a beat in Brooklyn and I'd make out all right.

"You came back today," he said. "To get this drawing he had made of you day before yesterday. When you heard he was dead you came back to get the sketch. Why?"

"It's mine. He hadn't paid me for it. Two hours and being yelled at. And ––"

"Yes," Shapiro said. "I understand how you feel. What did you plan to do with it, Miss Farmer?"

"What do you think, mister? Or are you a captain or something?"

"Lieutenant," Shapiro said, and there was sad acceptance in his voice. "You planned to sell it? Somebody would have bought it, you thought?"

She looked surprised at that. She had fixed her expression to superior detachment, or tried to. When he asked her that last question detachment melted out of her face. Her surprise was, Shapiro thought, almost childlike.

"Look," she said, and she was patient with the ignorant, with the outsider. "It's the last thing he did, isn't it? And you say, would somebody have *bought* it." She shook her head and the black hair swayed with the head's movement. "He used to get maybe two-three hundred for sketches. When he was willing to sell them. Of course, he only sold the ones he himself didn't like very much, when he needed money. He would now, I guess. I mean, if he hadn't killed himself and that's the last thing ––"

She stopped on that and shook her head again. It was easy enough to finish. It was, she was saying by not saying, the last thing she would have expected of Shackleford Jones.

"The others?"

"He just kept them. Things he really liked a lot he wouldn't even let people see. Anybody who might buy them, I mean. Myra Dedek used to send people down to look at things. Museum directors and people like that. And he'd show them only the things he didn't like, himself. And Myra would blow her top. You can't really blame her, I guess. A dealer's got to sell things, doesn't she?"

Involuntarily, Shapiro looked again around the loft, with pictures everywhere. He looked back at the tall young woman.

"People did buy his st–paintings? For hundreds of dollars?"

He heard the incredulity in his own voice. And when she answered, he heard incredulity in hers.

"Hundreds?" she repeated. "Are you out of your mind, mister?"

Nathan Shapiro thought it very likely. Or that the world was. Of course, the dark girl probably was making up a story. People do, sometimes for no special reason, when they talk to the police.

"You mean," Shapiro said, and spoke carefully, "that people paid more than hundreds?"

"You don't know much about this sort of thing, do you?" she asked him.

He shook his head. He said, "How much more?"

"Listen," she said, "I didn't keep books for him. Ask Myra Dedek. She did. And how she did! Fifty-fifty."

None of which made any particular sense to Lieutenant Nathan Shapiro.

"What he said . . ." the girl said, and reached back toward the easel, apparently to extract another of the thumbtacks which held the drawing.

"No," Shapiro said, and there was policeman in his voice. She removed her fingers from the tack they had started to fidget with.

" 'What he said'?" Shapiro repeated.

"They say he asked a lot," Rachel Farmer told him. "Asked crazy prices. Once he had a painting he insured for a hundred thousand dollars when it was being moved to Myra's gallery. Of course, it was a big painting. Ever so big. They had to take it out of here with a derrick or something. A piano–what do they use to move pianos?"

"From this high up, a hoist," Shapiro told her, and spoke as if he talked to the sane. "You're telling me Mr. Jones thought somebody might pay–" he steadied his voice– "a hundred thousand dollars for one of his paintings?"

"It was a big one," the girl said. "The biggest he ever did, I guess. Of course . . ."

She paused and Shapiro waited.

"I don't suppose," she said, "he really expected to get that much. He did put crazy prices on things he didn't really want to sell. But, then, he did think he was as good as Picasso. Or maybe almost."

"Have you any idea how much he would have taken for this picture? This very big picture?"

"Half of what he insured it for. I don't know. Sometimes he talked sort of wild. Lots of them do, you know."

Shapiro did not know. He thought it probable. Anything that afternoon was as probable as anything else.

"Myra sold one of the others–one he didn't like much–for ten thousand," the girl said. "Anyway, he said that. And he showed me the check. That was last fall. Of course, it was only for five thousand. He yelled about that. He was always yelling about Myra."

Shapiro steadied himself as well as he could.

"This one he sold," he said. "Do you know what it was about?"

Again there was astonishment in her face.

"About?" she said, and incredulity was in her voice. "*About?* Paintings aren't *about* things."

"They put titles on pictures, don't they?" Shapiro said. "There's one against the wall called 'Still Life.'"

"He called lots of them that," she said. "They all do."

"This one he told you was sold for ten thousand dollars?"

"Oh," she said. "That one. 'Composition in Planes' he called that one."

III

SHAPIRO TOLD RACHEL FARMER he would take her key to the studio. There was sulkiness in her face and she looked at the sketch she had come to get–come to steal. Which would have been grand larceny if her guess at its value was anything like true. Which it, of course, was not.

She said, "It's mine, really," and Shapiro said, "No. Let's have the key, Miss Farmer."

She did not carry a handbag, which was strange, but no stranger than anything else about all this. She fished into a pocket of her tight-fitting slacks and, after a slight struggle–she could not really get her hand into the pocket, so tightly did the slacks mold her–produced a ring with two keys on it. She started to separate the ring to take one of the keys off and Shapiro made a guess.

"The other one?" he said. "To his apartment, isn't it?"

Her expression told him he was right. She said, "Is it any of your business?"

"Perhaps not," Shapiro told her. "But I'll take them both," and then to Cook, "You've got her address, Tony?"

Cook said, "Yeah," with finality, and in a special voice experienced policemen keep available. The tone was not really threatening.

"We may want to ask you some more questions," Shapiro said. "You weren't planning a trip or anything like that?"

She shook her head and looked again at the drawing of the plucked ostrich. Shapiro again said, "No, Miss Farmer." He could not, actually, see why she would want it. He looked at it again himself. Her story about selling it was obviously a made-up story. But, as obviously, she wanted it, for whatever reason. Which was reason enough not to let her have it.

"You said you have an appointment," he said. "You can go along and keep it."

"You can't order me–" she said, and stopped with that and for a moment looked hard at him and again her expression seemed to him almost childlike; the expression of a resentful and uncertain child. Then she turned and took long strides to the door. She closed it after her with a bang.

"Funny way she has of walking," Cook said. "Like a man almost."

"I don't think so," Shapiro said, and did not have to explain what he did not think. "Skinny, but girl enough. Reason she had a key to his apartment, could be."

"Next stop?"

"May as–" Shapiro began and stopped. Precinct was ahead of them at the apartment, as it had been here at the studio–as, of course, it was everywhere. It was a nuisance to start hours behind. As long as they had to, they might start as nearly as they could at the beginning. At the moment, Shackleford Jones was an abstraction of a man. That could, to a degree, be remedied.

"Let's," Shapiro said, "go have a look at this cadaver of ours, Tony."

Across town and uptown to the morgue. Cook fumbled their way to Eighth Street. He drove slowly because traffic was moving slowly.

Shapiro had opportunity to look at Eighth Street, which was not much like anything he had seen before. Most of the men and women–and, obviously, the in-betweens–who walked the sidewalks between Sixth Avenue and Fifth seemed to be young, except when they were evidently very old. A heavy woman who walked a heavy dog was one of the old ones. She moved slowly, with numerous dog stops, and the younger swirled around her.

They swirled in twos, for the most part. They were in slacks, for the most part, and nobody wore a hat. Many of the males–the movements of hips identified the sexes, but some who were presumably female moved as stridingly as Rachel Farmer–were bearded. Some had achieved beards of stature. The less fortunate had wispy beards. They had, for the most part, made up for that by letting their hair grow long.

"Takes all kinds, like they say," Cook said, with the police car stopped in the narrow street to let a car ahead back into a parking space. "There's a pair for you."

He indicated the pair. Male and female from the way they moved. Yes, one of them with a beard. A red beard. He wore purple slacks. The other had no beard and walked somewhat as a woman walks. She wore green slacks into which, it was to be assumed, she had been poured.

The one with the beard walked with an arm about the other's shoulders. As the police car began to edge forward, the couple stopped and, with enthusiasm, kissed. Nobody else walking the sidewalks of the main street of Greenwich Village paid any attention to this. A Negro man and a white girl who had been walking behind the two who now clung so resolutely together swerved around the parked couple without breaking stride. As adeptly, they avoided a baby carriage, which a man in a red shirt and shorts and sandals was wheeling toward Sixth Avenue. There was a baby in the carriage. With the baby there were two large paper bags and from one of the bags a cabbage bulged. Two men walked behind him, both young. One of them, Shapiro was almost certain, had rouge on his lips.

Except for the people, Shapiro thought, Eighth Street here was the cluttered Main Street of a smallish town. There were grocery stores on either side, and liquor stores. On a corner there was a bookshop and it was crowded. A little beyond it, as they crept toward Fifth, there was, a flight below street level, "LeRoy's Gallery" and in the window which Shapiro could peer down into, a picture which looked, in the glimpse he had of it, like something from Shackleford Jones's studio. Above the gallery there was a Chinese restaurant. A man who wore a business suit and a straw hat and carried an attaché case led a clipped white poodle down the stairs from the Chinese restaurant. He opened the door of a Cadillac parked in front of the restaurant and the poodle jumped into it.

They came to Fifth and the lights stopped them. A nursemaid

in white uniform crossed Eighth, and held the hand of a small child in each of her hands. One of the children was a girl of five or six in a dress which was shiningly white; the other a boy, perhaps a little older, in a long-trousered blue business suit and a carefully tied blue four-in-hand. A Negro boy in blue jeans threw a ball over their heads and ran past them and almost caught it on the fly. But a bearded man of sixty or so really caught it and made a little bow and handed it to the Negro boy.

Across Fifth, at the corner, in a drive which curved from street into a towering apartment building, a uniformed chauffeur held the door of a limousine open for a billowy woman who wore white gloves almost to her elbows and a black dress which reached almost to her ankles. She wore a round black hat on very white hair. If it took all kinds, Shapiro thought, this was the place to find them.

They went on through Eighth Street and still went slowly. A derrick hoisting steel girders narrowed the roadway to a single lane and the building which the girders were to form was already a dozen stories tall and evidently going taller. Across the street from it there was a row of four low houses, dull red and sedate and old and each had a roof skylight facing toward the north.

"Lived in that one," Cook said, and pointed toward one of the old houses. Nathan Shapiro had seen the street number and said "Yes. We'll come back and have a look, Tony." There was a police cruise car parked in front of the house and, behind it, a precinct squad car. A trim woman in a dark blue silk suit was walking west on that side of the street. She stopped in front of the house, which was the second of the four from Fifth, and looked up at it. Then she walked on toward Fifth.

They turned uptown and, with the Village behind him, Cook drove with confidence. He found a place to put the car—a place marked *Official Use Only*—and, after identification and a moderate lapse of time, a man in a white uniform pulled a drawer open for them. The pathologists had not yet got around to taking Shackleford Jones apart to see what had made him stop ticking. But that was clear enough when the cadaver was turned to one side so that they could see the back of its head.

He had been a substantial man, solidly built. "Five-eleven, hundred and ninety," the morgue attendant told them. His body was deeply tanned, except where shorts had covered it. Sun beating down on him somewhere had burned his forehead dark. But, by comparison, his cheeks were almost pale. Shapiro puzzled over this for a moment and made a guess. When he had lain in the sun, absorbing its rays into his skin, Shackleford Jones had worn a beard. When he had come back from wherever he had been, from wherever there had been sunshine to lie in, Jones had shaved off his beard.

Jones had had blue eyes. He had had rather a heavy jaw. He had had strong, square hands. They looked, Shapiro thought, like the solid hands of a workman. Vaguely, Shapiro had expected thin hands with tapering fingers. He had expected a thin and tapering man, not this solid, rugged man. One makes up his mind as to what a man who does certain things in his life should look like, Shapiro thought. But men do not really fit the images one forms of them. Type-casting is, he thought, limited to the stage. The body of Shackleford Jones did not fit what Shackleford Jones had been.

Had been, at a guess, until he was somewhere in his middle forties. He had had sandy hair, and it had been thick healthy hair. He had had an appendectomy, probably some years before. He was short the little toe on his right foot. The muscles of his right arm were well developed. He looked, Shapiro thought, as if he might have played squash. He did not look like a man who would shoot himself in the back of the head.

The last thought was, of course, a ridiculous one. Men are no more type-cast for suicide than for occupation. At a guess, Shackleford Jones had not killed himself because he was a sick man; a man already dying slowly and unwilling to wait death out. But guessing about that was not in the province of Lieutenant Nathan Shapiro. The autopsy would decide that.

"We know what he looked like, anyway," Cook said, as they walked toward the car. "He looked husky enough."

There was that, for what it was worth. Shapiro could not see that it was worth much of anything. He found a booth and used a telephone.

Precinct had finished with the apartment. Papers found there had been bundled up and were being gone over. Shackleford Jones had had a passport. From the passport, it appeared he had recently been in Spain. He had had a checking account at the Sheridan Square office of the Chemical Bank New York Trust Company. The most recent statement showed a balance a little under four thousand dollars. But the statement dated back for more than three weeks. Jones had not balanced his checkbook for almost two weeks. When he had, previously, he had made several errors in addition. He had paid his rent for the loft in Little Great Smith Street and had a canceled check to prove it. (Amount, eighty-five dollars.) He had paid the Upton Realty Corporation two hundred and fifty dollars shortly after the first of the month, according to a stub entry. The stub said merely "Upton." A telephone directory and patience had produced the rest. The two hundred and fifty was the month's rental on the apartment in East Eighth Street. Jones had lived in it for two and a half years. He had paid his rent punctually.

The papers which had been bundled up did not include a will. Which proved nothing, since sensible people customarily leave their wills with the lawyers who draw them. Of course, sensible people also balance their checkbooks. Jones had had an account in the West Side Savings Bank. It totaled two thousand seven hundred and fifteen dollars and ninety-five cents.

The papers had not included a suicide note. One had been looked for.

The apartment, unlike the studio, apparently had been cleaned regularly. Jones's own fingerprints were in it, where one would have expected them to be—on chairs and tables, on his desk and his portable typewriter. There were prints of others, none on record in New York and all coded to Washington. "Looks like he had a cleaning woman in a couple of times a week, according to the f-p boys," Lieutenant Jacobs told Lieutenant Shapiro. "How're the brain boys doing, Nate?"

Homicide South was, to Lieutenant Jacobs, populated by brain boys.

"Puttering," Shapiro said. "Looking at the cadaver. Big one, isn't it, Jake?"

Jacobs admitted it was a big one. Anyway, a pretty big one.

"Which," Jacobs said, "doesn't prove a damn thing, does it, Nate? You still think somebody cooled him? You and the doc?"

He was being patient, Shapiro thought.

"Nothing to show he didn't cool himself," Shapiro said, agreeing. "But it came through 'suspicious,' Jake. So . . ."

He shrugged thin shoulders to go with the hanging "So."

At the apartment in East Eighth Street Shapiro used the key he had taken from Rachel Farmer. The long living room they went into was very unlike the studio in which Shackleford Jones had died. This room was carpeted in pale green. The carpet had a deep pile, recently trodden by many feet. There was a fireplace on one side of the room. It had not recently been used; had been carefully cleaned after its last use. But it was blackened by many fires. Against the wall opposite the fireplace there was a long sofa, deeply cushioned, covered in a material striped in deep yellow and soft white. At either end of it were chairs which looked comfortable, and did not look like each other.

There were a good many pictures on the living-room walls, which were painted pale yellow. But here pictures did not rush at one; here they were at peace against the yellow walls—the just yellow walls. Not, Shapiro thought, that they were of themselves peaceful pictures. These, like those in the studio, had jagged shapes and flagrant colors. But here they seemed at home; seemed to have intent. No more than before could Shapiro fathom their intent. They were not, so far as he could see, "about" anything. Probably the Farmer girl was right; probably they were not supposed to be. But still . . .

The framed canvas which hung above the fireplace was, when he looked at it first, like the others—a painting of shapes and colors, saying nothing. But then, as he continued to look at it, it became oddly comprehensible. The shapes and colors formed into the head and shoulders of a man—shaped themselves so, lost that shape, resumed that shape. Then, quite suddenly, the face they disjointedly hinted at became a familiar face.

This painting was, whatever the Farmer girl said, "about" something. This painting was about Shackleford Jones, deceased. Shapiro walked over to it and looked at the small metal plate set into the frame. "Self portrait" was etched on the plate. And in the lower right-hand corner of the canvas there was the now familiar "Shack." Shapiro experienced a moment of self-congratulation, and instantly rejected it.

"Could do with some light in here," Cook said, from deeper in the long room.

Daylight came through two windows, curtained in pale green, at one end of the room. It was true that not a great deal of light came through them, although they reached from floor to ceiling. Shapiro, who was nearest it, flicked up a switch by the door. Three lamps went on softly in the long room and one under the self portrait threw light up against the canvas. The picture changed as the light fell on it. It took life from the light.

There was a closed door in the right-hand wall beyond the fireplace. Shapiro turned the knob and pushed the door open and brushed his hands together to rid them of fingerprint dust. He stood in a bedroom, unexpectedly large–large enough to hold a double bed comfortably. There was a clothes chest in the room; a door opened to a closet. The late Shackleford Jones had had a good many clothes and had kept them neatly hung. Another door opened to a bathroom. The tub in it had recently been polished.

The bedroom was better lighted, now in late afternoon, than the living room had been. The light came through tall French doors which could be opened onto a tiny balcony above a back-yard garden. Shapiro looked through the glass and, momentarily, watched a black and white cat climbing a high board fence. The cat jumped against the fence and appeared to walk up it. When he reached the top of the fence he sat down and looked around, Shapiro supposed, for another cat.

Jones had lived comfortably in East Eighth Street. Perhaps, some weeks earlier, there had been tulips in the garden he could look down on.

Shapiro went back into the living room. Cook had opened folding doors at the end of it. The doors, closed, concealed a kitchen. It was, as kitchens go in old houses which have been converted to apartments, large. Its equipment was compact. One could stand at the sink and look through a window and, again, look down at the garden. Shapiro looked. The cat, now, was crouched on top of the fence. Perhaps he had seen another cat.

There was an electric range in the kitchen and, above it, an exhaust fan was set into the wall. The range looked new. So did the refrigerator opposite it. For no special reason, Shapiro opened the refrigerator door.

There was a good deal of food in the refrigerator–bread and eggs and butter; in "crisper" bins below the main storage area, oranges and lemons and a head of romaine. In the main compartment were bottles of gin and vermouth and rum. There was also, on its side, a bottle of champagne. There were four small birds wrapped, professionally, in cellophane. Shapiro took one of the birds out and read the wrapper. He read: "Meadow Hill Squab." In smaller type he read: "Keep frozen until ready to use." The squab was cold; it was not frozen.

Rose did not use much food from a freezer. When she did she sometimes took what she planned to use from the freezer a few hours beforehand, to let the thawing begin. Shapiro put the squab back with the others and said, "Hm-m-m" to which Cook said, "Find something?"

Shapiro pointed into the refrigerator and Cook crouched and peered into it. He said, "Did himself all right, didn't he?" and stood up and looked at Shapiro and raised his eyebrows.

"Squabs," Shapiro said and pointed at them. "Frozen, but taken out of the freezing section. Not this morning. He was dead this morning. Yesterday, it could be, couldn't it, Tony? Planned to roast them last night, could be, couldn't it? For a guest, probably. Two squabs each and half a bottle of champagne each. And a salad. Everything all ready and planned, wouldn't you say, Tony? By a man who expected to eat squab and, perhaps, toast a lady friend."

The refrigerator clicked and began to whir. Shapiro closed the lower door and reopened the freezer compartment. There were six ice-cube trays in it, all full of ice. There were four long-stemmed cocktail glasses standing on the freezing plate beside the trays. There was also a can of frozen daiquiri mix.

"Liked his martinis cold," Shapiro said. "Could be, of course, that the daiquiri was to have been for him and the martinis for his guest. Two chilled glasses for each of them."

He tugged gently at one of the cocktail glasses. It was frozen in. So were the others. So was the can of daiquiri mix.

"Same type icebox Rose and I've got at home," Shapiro said, speaking as much to himself as to Detective Anthony Cook. "Defrosts once every twenty-four hours at the time you set it for." He looked at this refrigerator's dial. "Two in the morning he set it for," Shapiro said. "Two in the morning the freezing plate would warm up and the ice on it melt and the water run off. Supposed to, anyway. Doesn't always with ours. Run off, I mean."

Cook listened. He was patient about it. A detective, even first grade, listens when a lieutenant talks. Even when the lieutenant doesn't seem to be getting much of anywhere.

"Freezer goes back on," Shapiro said, "and anything standing on the plate freezes to it. Have to defrost to get things loose again." He ran fingers over the ice which had formed on the metal freezer plate. It was not, he thought, very thick around the bases of the glasses, where it would have held. At a guess, the glasses had frozen in at two o'clock that morning. Shapiro closed the door of the freezing compartment.

"See the way it looks, don't you?" Shapiro said. "Left here yesterday morning and went over to that studio of his to paint one of those things of his. And expected to be back here for dinner, wouldn't you say? Sort of a party dinner. Expected to be alive to eat it, didn't he?"

"Could be he made up his mind all at once," Cook said. He considered this. "I guess it could," he said, with doubt.

"Sure," Shapiro said. "Probably I'm making too much out of nothing much. Habit of mine, my wife tells me. Of course, bits and pieces are what they've left us."

He sighed. Probably Cook was right. No one could tell what

went on in the mind of a man before he killed himself. Shapiro would have thought an act so final was one to think about for a considerable time. Shackleford Jones, even on a morgue slab, had looked like a man who enjoyed living; one who would have been tempted to life by a cold bottle of champagne and the crisp succulence of roasted squabs. His thoughts were idle, as usually they were, Nathan Shapiro told himself. Still ––

They turned simultaneously at the sound–the sound of key grating in lock, the click of the lock's tongue snapping from its striking plate. The door hinges squeaked a little as the door was pushed open. For an instant, looking up the room, Shapiro expected to see Rachel Farmer walking thinly into it.

He did not. This woman walked with confidence, as the Farmer girl had. She, too, apparently expected to find the room unoccupied. But this woman was small and trim. She wore a blue silk suit and carried a handbag which matched the suit. She moved into the room with quick grace on high-heeled blue shoes, which also matched the suit.

She moved so for only a few quick steps and then stopped and looked at the sconce light under the picture. She had not expected to find the room lighted, Nathan Shapiro guessed. She looked down the room.

Nothing, this time, hid Shapiro and Cook. And nothing hid from them the tall man who followed the trim woman into the room. He wore a polo shirt and gray slacks and, somewhat unexpectedly to Shapiro, sandals. He had a pointed beard which, from the distance, looked well tended. He carried a long screwdriver in his right hand.

"Who," the woman said, "are you two? And what are you doing here?"

She had a clear, incisive voice. It kept its incisiveness for the length of the room.

"Police," Shapiro said, and he and Cook began to walk toward the woman and the man, who swayed the screwdriver back and forth in his hand as if he felt there were something he ought to do with it. "And you, miss?"

"Myra Dedek," the woman said. "It's Mrs. Dedek. I thought all of you had finished here."

That, Shapiro thought, was reasonably obvious. He said, "Just about, Mrs. Dedek," and thought that if it had been a shock to her to find a painter named Jones lying dead on the floor, with congealed blood around him, she had bounced back from shock. She looked like a woman who would bounce back. Her almost unlined face was firm, decisive as her voice. Her black hair waved obediently on her small, precise head. She looked a little, but not too much, as if she had just come from a beauty salon.

"What do you expect to find here?" she asked, and now there was a little impatience in her voice. "The poor man killed himself. Is that a crime?"

In New York suicide is a violation of the penal code. There was no use, at the moment, going into that.

"Routine," Shapiro said sadly. "There's always routine, Mrs. Dedek. Forms have to be filled out."

She shrugged neat shoulders. She said, "In poor Shack's kitchen? Or are the two of you just hungry?"

An aggressive woman, Shapiro thought. For any special reason aggressive? Or merely so by nature? Ran a picture gallery uptown. Seventy-ninth Street off Madison. Had gone to the studio that morning to talk with Jones about a one-man show set for the next fall. To find out what he had that he had not shown before. What he had done in Spain during the previous winter. Had a key because he wasn't always there and she was seldom free to waste her time.

She had still been crying when the first policemen reached the studio in Little Great Smith Street. She had regained composure quickly. She had been succinct and reasonable. She had not seen Shackleford Jones for more than a week; had snatched the first moment she had free. No, she had not telephoned before she went to the studio. "He hated the telephone. Most of the time he didn't answer it." She had been downtown, anyway; had decided it would be a good time to drop in on Jones. If he wasn't there, a good time to look at his new things, if there were new things, without his fussing around about it.

She had knocked at the studio door and there had been no answer. She had used her key and opened the door. From the doorway, she had seen Jones lying face down on the studio floor, with congealed blood around him. She had screamed, at first involuntarily, because of what she saw. She was shaking as she told the first policeman about this; her body shook and her voice shook.

Then, without going farther into the room, she had screamed down the stairs for help.

Her questioning had been brief. She was Myra Dedek. She had a gallery in East Seventy-ninth Street and an apartment above it. If they wanted her to go over it again, and she supposed they would (although what had happened was certainly clear enough) they could get in touch with her at her apartment.

There had been no reason not to let her go to her apartment, or wherever she wanted to go. She had walked in on an ugly thing, Detective James O'Brien had realized. There was no use in prolonged questioning of a woman obviously under strain, however she tried to hide it, at a moment when there were other things to do.

That, Shapiro remembered from his briefing in the early afternoon. He agreed that there had been no point in keeping her hanging around. Now he looked down at her and then, at a level, at the man with her. Younger than she was, by the looks of him.

"Weldon Williams," the young man said, without being asked. "An assistant of Mrs. Dedek's." He continued to wave the screwdriver gently in his right hand.

"What do you plan to do with that?" Shapiro asked him.

The bearded man looked at Myra Dedek, obviously for guidance.

"Take that down, of course," Mrs. Dedek said. She pointed at the painting above the fireplace. "I think I have a buyer for it. It's fixed in with toggle bolts, so we'll need a screwdriver."

She was entirely matter of fact. She spoke as if her intention to walk into the apartment of a dead man and take his pictures off the wall was an obviously reasonable one. It was increasingly a day when nothing was particularly comprehensible to Lieutenant Nathan Shapiro.

"Just like that?" Shapiro said.

She didn't, she said, know what he meant.

"You and Mr. Williams planned to walk into Mr. Jones's apartment and take his pictures off the wall. And, apparently, sell them if somebody wants to buy them. What makes you think you can do that, Mrs. Dedek?"

"Why shouldn't I?" she said. "Heaven knows anything I can salvage–what's your name, by the way? I don't like to talk to people whose names I don't know. All I know is that you say you're the police."

Shapiro gave her his name and showed her his badge. He told her Cook's name and Cook showed her his badge. She looked at both badges carefully. Shapiro suspected she was memorizing the numbers on them.

"Seem to be all right," she admitted. "Though why it's any of your business."

"Death by violence," Shapiro said, and let patience sound clearly in his voice. "Always business of the police, Mrs. Dedek. What do you mean, salvage?"

"Get my money back is what I mean," the trim, decisive woman said, and let impatience sound in her voice. "What did you think I meant? Take the picture down, Weldon. Don't stand there like a ninny."

Weldon Williams looked uncertainly at Lieutenant Shapiro. Shapiro resolved his uncertainty by saying, "No."

"Suppose you explain what you mean," Shapiro said to Mrs. Dedek, who said, "To you?"

"To my superiors, if you'd rather have it that way," Shapiro said. "Mean a trip across town. Maybe down to headquarters. Maybe to the district attorney's office."

"A lot of fuss about nothing," Myra Dedek said. "But, all right. If you insist on being officious."

She went to the long sofa which faced the fireplace and sat on it and put her handbag on the coffee table in front of it. Shapiro went over and stood in front of her and watched her open the bag. He could look down into it; could watch her fingers move certainly for what she wanted. There was not any jumble in the handbag. She did not need to paw through it, stir anxiously through it, as women usually stir through handbags. Her fingers went at once to a pocket in the bag and came out with a folded sheet of paper.

Not as naive as she had pretended, Shapiro thought. She had come prepared. She handed him the sheet of paper and he unfolded it. Very neatly typed, the passage he read was. Electric typewriter. He read:

"I hereby authorize Mrs. Myra Dedek, of —— East Seventy-ninth Street, New York City, in the event of my death, to sell such paintings of mine as may be necessary to realize a sum sufficient to reimburse her for cash advances she has made to me over past years. After she has recovered the amount due her, I authorize her to continue the sale and, after deducting her customary percentage, to pay the residue to my estate."

It was signed "Shackleford Jones," and the signature had been notarized. The notarization was dated three years ago the previous November.

When he had finished reading, she held a hand out and said, "Satisfied?" But he did not put the again folded paper into the hand held out for it. He gave it to Cook to read. When Cook had read it, he looked at Shapiro and raised his eyebrows.

"Give Mrs. Dedek a receipt for it," Shapiro told him.

Myra Dedek pushed herself violently from the sofa. She said, "You can't do that! You haven't any right to. My lawyer ——"

"You'll get it back," Shapiro said. "See your lawyer by all means, Mrs. Dedek. I'll sign the receipt, Tony."

Tony Cook tore out of his notebook a sheet on which he had written, "Received from Mrs. Myra Dedek a notarized document purporting to be an authorization to sell paintings by Shackleford Jones, dec." He dated it. Nathan Shapiro signed it. He gave it to the trim dark-haired woman and for a moment he thought she was going to tear it up. But she put it in her handbag. She said, "You'll be sorry about this, Lieutenant."

Shapiro thought that quite possible, but did not say so. He

might well be exceeding his authority, which was to clean up odds and ends after a suicide. If, of course, this was suicide. Murder would make it quite another matter.

"The advances he mentions," Shapiro said. "Want to tell me about those, Mrs. Dedek?"

"I don't have to tell you anything."

Shapiro answered, first, with a sigh. Then he said, "No, you don't have to tell me anything. That's quite right. You and Mr. Williams can go any time you like. Without taking any pictures with you."

"If I —"

"No. You still can't take the pictures. Not now. With this–" he waggled the authorization Cook had given back to him and then put it in a jacket pocket–"you'll probably get them. But you'll have to do it legally. You did advance Mr. Jones money?"

"For years. There's not really a secret about it. A good many dealers . . ."

All at once, she was willing to talk. It was possible, Shapiro thought, that she had come prepared to talk, if she needed to.

A good many dealers advanced money to painters who, they thought, might eventually sell, on the reasonable assumption that a promising painter will be more productive if he doesn't starve to death. It was a gamble, obviously. As often as not it was a losing gamble. Sometimes it paid off.

"It's all a gamble," she said. "We set up a gallery and that costs money. We keep it running. Pay the rent. We show paintings and sell them and get our percentage. *If* we sell them."

"You sold Jones's paintings?"

"Some of them. Five years ago it looked as if he was a comer. Recently —" She spread her hands to finish the sentence.

"Not so good?"

"Not at the ridiculous prices he set on things. Anyway —" This time she shrugged her shoulders. Shapiro waited.

IV

NATHAN SHAPIRO SAT in one of the chairs by the sofa and Anthony Cook sat in the other and made notes. Weldon Williams, his sandals flapping slightly, walked around the room and looked at the pictures on the walls. He continued to dangle the screwdriver.

Myra Dedek let her "anyway" hang for more than a minute, while, Shapiro thought, she considered it.

"I may as well tell you what I think," she said, after the long pause. This was an introductory statement which Shapiro had seldom found convincing, but she looked at him from almost black eyes, as if for response. He nodded his head and said, "Do that, Mrs. Dedek."

She said, "You'll spread it around. Could be I'm cutting my own throat."

There was nothing to say to that because, to Shapiro, it was a meaningless remark.

"Ten years ago," Myra Dedek said, "I could have sworn he was a comer. Not another Motherwell. I don't say that. Not as good as he thought he was. Not by miles. But . . . good. Good enough to invest in. You see what I mean?"

"To make cash advances to," Shapiro said, to show that he followed. He did not, entirely. "Not another Motherwell" got him nowhere.

"Of course," Myra Dedek said. "I gave him his first one-man show. Did you know that?"

"No," Shapiro said, and forebore to ask, "Was that good?"

"Style," the slim, dark woman said. "Originality. Oh, you could see derivations. I don't argue you couldn't see who had influenced him. But a real talent. A talent to bet on. And did I bet on it! Didn't I just."

"How much?" It wasn't, he supposed, really any of his business. But it was impossible to tell what was his business.

"Fifty thousand dollars," she said. "Five thousand a year for ten years."

Involuntarily, Nathan Shapiro looked around the big, well-furnished room. He thought of champagne in the refrigerator. He thought of the air conditioning in the loft studio, which must have cost plenty. He tried to fit these things together with five thousand a year.

"These payments," he said. "They were advances, I gather? Against what he might sell. He didn't sell?"

"Some things. Particularly at first."

"You charged what he got–would have got–against the money you advanced?"

"A percentage. Not all of it. I was soft about that." Shapiro waited. "All right," she said, "I thought he would work better if I kept him happy. He raved and ranted. Anybody will tell you that. But underneath, he wasn't certain. Underneath, he wasn't sure. They're like that, some of them. You have to keep on telling them they're wonderful."

They seemed, Shapiro thought, to be going off on a tangent. But he had no way of knowing, in this tangential day, what was a tangent and what was not. He sought more solid ground.

"When he sold a picture through your gallery," Shapiro said. "The buyer would pay how much, Mrs. Dedek?"

"A thousand sometimes. Once or twice twenty-five hundred. That was before he began to ask those exorbitant prices."

"He fixed the prices?"

"Oh," she said, "we argued about them. But he didn't have to sell through me, you know. Anyway, when he wanted outrageous prices, it was because he didn't really want to sell some of his paintings. He just wanted to keep them and look at them himself."

That was a tangent Shapiro recognized. Rachel Farmer had said much the same thing. It hadn't made much sense when she said it, either. He worked back toward the tangible.

"Say you sold one of his pictures for a thousand dollars," Shapiro said. "What part of it would he get?"

"As a dealer," she said, "I take half of what a picture sells for. With most of them, anyway. You've no idea what my overhead is. You ——" But then she looked at him intently and said, "What business is all this of yours, Lieutenant? The poor man shot himself. You know that."

"It looks that way," Shapiro said. "Helps if we can find out what makes a man kill himself. You see, we have to be certain that he did. Always a chance what looks like suicide isn't."

"And go around getting people who knew him to talk about him?"

"Comes to that. This thousand somebody paid for one of his paintings. You got five hundred. He got–how much? How much did you charge off against what he owed you?"

"Half of his share. Two-fifty."

Five thousand a year in advances. Occasional sales with half of his share deducted. Shapiro looked around the room again, and this time made it obvious. Not that he thought things needed to be made obvious to this sharp-eyed and probably sharp-witted woman. This woman who, after having started with antagonism, had suddenly turned talkative.

"All right," she said. "He sold some things on his own. Some of his early things. He was free to do that. That was understood. As long as it was not through another dealer."

"You know a Miss Farmer? Miss Rachel Farmer?"

"She posed for him. Posed for several others, too. Slept with him, for all I know. Or with all of them. What's she got to do with it?"

"She says," Shapiro told her, "that you recently sold one of his paintings for ten thousand. That he told her that. And that he showed her a check for five thousand. His share."

"He had the nerve to tell her that?"

"What she says. It wasn't true?"

"Never. I never–wait a minute. When was this? Did she say?"

"Last autumn."

"He told her *that?*" The incredulity was stressed.

"Yes," Shapiro said. "It wasn't true?"

"The five thousand–yes, that was true enough. Only, it was my last bet. Throwing good money after bad. I may as well tell you, I suppose. You want to know why he killed himself, don't you? That's what all this is about, you say."

"Yes."

"He was painted out," she said. "And he knew it. He'd been to his analyst, of course. Even that hadn't helped. Oh, he still kept on painting. But the last two or three years he's been repeating himself. The vigor went out of everything. No new conceptions. You understand what I mean?"

Shapiro thought of the painting he had looked at in the studio, and didn't at all understand what she meant. But he said, "I think so, Mrs. Dedek."

"He came to me last fall and said he was going stale. And made a pitch. If I advanced him enough to spend the winter somewhere else, somewhere he could see different things and think different thoughts, it might turn the trick. He knew I'd already invested a good deal in him. He didn't want to leave me holding the bag. Apologetic as all hell, he was. Seen him like that before. Sounded sort of licked. So, all right, I turned soft. Myra Dedek–Myra Dedek of all people–got soft. Can you believe it?"

She did not appear to expect an answer, which was as well, since Nathan Shapiro had none ready.

"So," the black-haired trim woman said, "I gave him a check for five thousand so he could go to Spain and–refresh himself. That's the way he put it. 'Refresh' himself. And–all right. I thought something might come of it. And that we'd get back to selling Shacks. I don't deny I'm a business woman. Never have."

A woman touched by a man who sounded "licked." A woman who, all the same, thought there might be profit to be made by further investment–adding to a total of five thousand dollars? All this about colors smeared on canvas. Shapiro sighed.

"He went to Spain?"

"Yes."

"And been back how long?"

"About three weeks."

"Did it work? Or don't you know?"

"I know. No, it didn't work. He'd planned to stay a year, but it didn't work and he came back. Blamed Spain, of course."

"He told you that?"

"And showed me that. Oh, he'd done some things while he was in Spain. They weren't any better. Worse, if anything. Tired, familiar things. I couldn't say they weren't. Wouldn't have made any difference if I had, because he wasn't a fool. Just a man who had run through his talent and–hadn't anything left. Not anything at all." There was emphasis on the last words.

"You think that might have led him to kill himself?"

"I know it did. *Know* it did."

She leaned forward as she said this. Her small hands clenched into fists. Then, abruptly, she stood up and said, "Weldon!" and her voice was sharp. Weldon Williams, still with screwdriver in hand, wandered back into the room, apparently from the bedroom. Possibly, of course, from the bathroom.

"We're going," Myra Dedek told the lanky, bearded man. She turned to Shapiro sharply. "Any reason we shouldn't?" she asked him.

"No," Shapiro said. "You've been helpful. Oh–there's one other thing. Have you any idea who Mr. Jones might have planned to have here for dinner last night?"

She widened her eyes.

"What a ridiculous question," she said. "However would I know, Lieutenant Shapiro? I never had anything–*anything at all*–to do with his personal life."

She was very emphatic about it, Shapiro thought. Made an issue of it. Which a little made him wonder.

Weldon Williams came up the long room and went on toward the door. He still dangled the screwdriver. Mrs. Dedek went around the coffee table and started to join him.

"One more thing, Mrs. Dedek," Shapiro said. "Until everything gets cleared up, you'd better give me your key to this apartment. One of the rules is, we keep places locked up until we've finished."

He expected a protest, a further reference to her lawyer. He got neither; he got a key from her handbag. Then she joined the lanky, bearded man at the door. There she stopped and turned back.

"What makes you think he planned to have somebody here for dinner?" she asked.

He told her, briefly.

"That Rachel Farmer one," Mrs. Dedek said. "She's one for champagne, from what little I know of her. Go *on,* Weldon."

She went after Weldon Williams. It was she who closed the door behind them. She closed it with marked decision, although she did not really slam it.

"Gives us a motive, anyway," Cook said. "For Jones to kill himself."

"Yes," Shapiro said. "There's that, Tony. When we passed here earlier, on our way to the morgue, you happen to notice a woman who stopped in front of this building and looked up at it? And then went on?"

Cook had not. He had, he pointed out, had enough things to look at, what with the crane blocking most of the street.

"Mrs. Dedek, I think," Shapiro said. "Checking to see if the coast was clear. Deciding it wasn't. Police cars around."

"Well," Cook said, "fifty grand is a good deal of grand, isn't it?"

Shapiro agreed that it was. He said, "Let's see if we can find Gay Street, Tony."

Tony Cook looked at the watch on his wrist and, in sympathy, Nathan Shapiro looked at his own. It was almost six o'clock. The working hours even of policemen are stipulated, although the stipulation does not always hold. Quite probably, Tony Cook had a date. He was unmarried and of an age for dates. Shapiro himself thought wistfully of Brooklyn. If he left Gay Street for tomorrow, he could get home in time to walk the dog before he and Rose had dinner. If he said now, "O.K., Tony. Tomorrow will do," he and Rose could catch a movie. Probably Shackleford Jones had shot himself because he had "run through his talent."

In the back of the head? With squabs waiting, champagne chilling, in the refrigerator?

"You're pretty sure it wasn't suicide, aren't you?" Detective Anthony Cook said, in the car.

When a question waits an answer the answer sometimes helps.

"Yes," Shapiro said. "Aren't you, Tony?"

Cook worked the car from the curb into the only lane the towering crane left open in East Eighth Street. Then he answered.

"Yes," Cook said, "I guess I am, Lieutenant. Where the hell do you suppose Gay Street is?"

They went north in University Place, west in Ninth Street. At the tangle of streets where West Ninth encounters Sixth Avenue and gives the whole thing up, they found a traffic cop. When in doubt, ask a policeman. This one pointed and described.

Gay Street runs a crooked block between Christopher and Waverly Place. It is very narrow and one-way and barely that. There were signs which read: *No Parking Any Time*. Cook pulled the car half onto the sidewalk, behind a truck which did not believe in signs.

The building was a three-story one, and once had been a private house. On either side were taller buildings which had never been anything but tenements. There were buttons for three bells in the dim vestibule, and they had names in slots beside them. One of the names was "Rachel Farmer" and when the button was pushed there was a distant, buzzing sound. After a lapse of time there was a harsh and immediate buzzing which emanated from the door.

They climbed a flight of narrow stairs and found a door at the end of the corridor. There was no name on the door. Shapiro reached out to knock on it and it opened before he touched it. He looked down at the man who had jerked it open.

The man was slight and not much more than five feet tall. He had soft, yellow hair which, by Shapiro's prejudices, needed cutting, but which became the slender, blue-eyed man, who wore shorts and a polo shirt and who had the legs and the torso to suit both. Built like a featherweight in fine condition, Shapiro thought. Except that nobody had been hitting him in the face.

Shapiro said, "Miss Farmer in?"

"In," the man said. "But I doubt if she'll want whatever it is."

He had an unexpectedly deep voice. There was a suggestion of British clipping in his speech.

"Police," Shapiro said. "Want to ask —"

"About Shack Jones," the man said. "Apparently walked into something. Rache did. Like her, y'know."

He unhooked the guard chain and opened the door and turned to call, "Got company, my girl."

Then he walked away from them into a square room with floor to ceiling windows at the end of it.

Rachel Farmer stood on a wooden platform by one of the windows and had apparently been looking out of it. She turned to face the small graceful man and the two detectives and said, "You two again."

She seemed entirely unconcerned by the fact that she was wearing nothing at all. Naked, she seemed even taller than she had in black sweater and slacks. She had small, high breasts and a very slender waist and no hips to speak of and entirely admirable legs. She might walk like a man, Anthony Cook thought, but she certainly did not look like one.

"What do you want now?" Rachel Farmer asked, her tone entirely conversational.

"A few things have come up," Shapiro said. He paused. "If you want . . ." He hesitated.

"We know you've got a beautiful body, m'dear," the yellow-haired man said. "Put something on it, there's a girl." She looked at him in apparent surprise. "Embarrass your guests," the man told her. "Expect people to wear clothes, policemen do."

She said, "Oh–that," and looked down at herself. Then she said, "If you say so, Max," and stepped off the low platform and walked across the square room to an open door and went through the doorway. She was still unconcerned. She acceded gracefully to the prejudices of policemen.

"Posing for me," the yellow-haired man said. "Rather an abstracted type, at best. And used to nudity, of course." He shook his head, apparently at himself. "Mincing word, 'nudity,'" he said. "My name's Maxwell Briskie, by the way. Painter of sorts. Doing some sketches of Rache."

He pointed toward a chair which faced the platform on which Rachel Farmer had been standing. There was a drawing pad lying on the chair. "Here. I'll show you," Maxwell Briskie said, and walked across the room. He moved with quick grace. He came back with the sketch pad.

He had, in what Shapiro took to be charcoal, drawn a woman. Shapiro guessed he had drawn a woman. But the woman was attenuated beyond belief and even, for that matter, beyond Rachel Farmer. She appeared, also, to have two faces, pointed in different directions.

"Preliminary, of course," Briskie said. "Just roughed in. May not come to anything."

He is, Shapiro thought, amused. My expression, Shapiro thought, is no doubt amusing in its bafflement. But he did have her standing there so that he could draw a picture of her. She ––

Rachel Farmer came back through the door, which presumably led to her bedroom. She wore a thin silk robe, belted around her slender waist. It was obvious that she wore nothing else. She had only one face.

She walked to them, taking long strides, indifferent to the fact that with each stride the robe parted from long legs. She took the sketch pad from Maxwell Briskie and looked at the drawing. She said, "Watch it, Maxie. You're getting representational," and handed the pad back to him.

"And," she said, "you owe me ten dollars."

Briskie slapped a flat hip pocket of his shorts. He accentuated an expression of surprise at the negative result. She pointed with her left thumb toward the ceiling.

"And miss the fun and games?" Max Briskie said. "Not likely. Always wondered about the third degree." He looked at her reflectively. "Rubber hoses, I shouldn't wonder," he said. "Always brings out the sadist in me, m'dear."

She sighed, making a point of it.

"He's impossible," she said, and turned to Shapiro. "Always has been. What *do* you want now? If Shack's sketch is gone, somebody else took it. Anyway, you took my key."

"Two keys," Shapiro said. "To the studio. To the apartment. About the apartment. Did you plan to have dinner–or supper –with Mr. Jones there last night?"

"He was dead last night. Are you crazy, man?"

"Yes," Shapiro said. "He was dead last night. But perhaps he didn't plan to be, Miss Farmer. We rather think he was expecting a guest. Was it you?"

"No. I already had a date. With Mr. Lathrop Vance, if you want to know." She spoke the name as if it must inevitably have meaning. To Shapiro it had none. He said, "Did you keep the date, Miss Farmer?"

"If it's any of your business, yes. We went to the St. Regis. We danced. What made you think I'd get cooped up with poor old Shack? Watch him fuss around with his cooking?"

It was a day of tangents. Shapiro, tempted, took the one offered. He said, "He liked to cook?"

"He made a thing of it. He was–what's the word, Maxie? Goo something."

"Gourmet, I expect," Max Briskie said. "The old boy did spend a lot of time fiddling around in his kitchen. Spanish period since he got back from Spain a while back. Things with octopus in them, from what I hear. Have octopus in his frig, Captain?"

"Lieutenant," Shapiro said, and added the rest of it. "No. Squabs. And champagne."

The result of this was unexpected. The slim, graceful little man looked away from Shapiro and seemed to look into the distance. He said, "Hm-m-m. Squabs, was it?" as if the word "squabs" had some special meaning.

"Yes, Maxie," Rachel Farmer said. "The little birds Dotty does so well." There was, it seemed to Shapiro, amusement in her voice and, at the same time, sympathy. She turned from Max

Briskie and looked at Shapiro. She was of a height to look at him levelly.

"Does it matter who was going to have dinner with him last night? Or a late supper with him?"

"I don't know," Shapiro said. "I don't know at the moment what matters. We're just checking things out."

"You people go to a lot of trouble, don't you?" the tall dark girl said. "Because a man gets fed up with being alive. Or have the police got another idea, mister?"

Shapiro did not answer directly. He turned to Maxwell Briskie, who still seemed to be looking at something far away.

"You're a painter, Mr. Briskie," he said. "You knew Mr. Jones's work?"

For a moment, Briskie seemed to stay at whatever distant point he had gone to. But then he came back and looked up at Shapiro and said, "Yes. I knew Shack's work." He paused. "Some of it was rather good," he said, and paused again. "All right," he said, "a lot of it was damn good."

"Had it fallen off lately? I mean ——" He searched his memory. "Had he been repeating himself, would you say? Run out of new ideas?" "Ideas" was not the right word. He remembered. "Conceptions?" he said.

"Whatever gave you that idea?"

"Something somebody said."

"Somebody was nuts, Lieutenant. Last two or three years Shack was almost as good as he thought he was. Which says one hell of a lot. Somebody's pulling your leg, Lieutenant."

Shapiro did not doubt that somebody had. It would be interesting to find out who. He wasn't, of course, the man to find out. But he would have to have a try at it.

"Mrs. Dedek said something of the kind," Shapiro told them both. And Rachel Farmer said, "What it comes to, Myra's a square. A square bitch in a round hole."

Max Briskie's blue eyes narrowed as he looked up at the tall thin girl, and vertical lines appeared in his smooth, wide forehead.

"You don't agree, Mr. Briskie?" Shapiro said.

"That she's a bitch? No argument. But I'd say she knows her business. Which is knowing what collectors will buy."

"Have you asked dear Myra?" Rachel Farmer said, with evident meaning in her tone. But what the meaning was was not evident. So Nathan Shapiro said, "Asked her what, Miss Farmer?"

"If she was the guest you think Shack was expecting, of course."

She was impatient with him.

"Yes," Shapiro said. "She says she wasn't, Miss Farmer. And you say you weren't."

"Whoever it was," Max Briskie said, "didn't get to eat the squabs. Or drink the champagne. Heard that Shack was dead. It was all over this part of town. And in the afternoon papers. And on the radio. So considered it a broken date. What difference does it make?"

"I don't know that it makes any," Shapiro said. "We like to fill in all the gaps. What we're supposed to do, Detective Cook here and I."

"This," Briskie said, "is getting to be a dull do. You promised rubber hoses."

Shapiro managed to smile faintly as he shook his head. And he thought the flippancy forced, as it had not been before.

"So," Briskie said, "I'll go up and get your tenner, Rache, darling."

He turned as he spoke and walked toward the door. He had the balance of a featherweight fighter. He opened the door and went out, without looking back.

"Poor Maxie," Rachel Farmer said. "He lives upstairs, you know. He and his wife. Dorothy Goodbody, her professional name is. Almost a head taller than him. You've heard of her?"

Shapiro shook his head.

"Writes songs," Rachel Farmer said. "Some of them have gone over. I've been up to dinner with them a few times."

Nathan Shapiro was beginning to expect non sequiturs from the tall girl. He said, "Have you?"

"Three times, exactly," Rachel Farmer said. "Twice we had squabs. Dotty's very fond of squabs, mister."

V

It was late when Nathan Shapiro got home to Brooklyn, and walked familiar blocks from subway station to apartment building. But the day holds long in June, and the sunlight still slanted on the sidewalks. The people who walked the sidewalks were familiar people; were reasonable people, reasonably dressed. This did not, of course, mean that they were better people than the strangers on Eighth Street, Borough of Manhattan—more moral or necessarily more law-abiding or, come to that, more universally heterosexual. Shapiro said, "'Evening, Abe," to a swarthy round man who was, as everybody knew, a bookie. He did not say anything to, or even give a policeman's hard-eyed look at, Angelo Bertilotto, who was widely, and to the police unfavorably, known as "Bang-Bang Bertie." "Bang-Bang" was not, at the moment, wanted for anything.

He said, "'Evening, Rabbi" to Rabbi Isidore Goldberg of the congregation of which he was himself a not particularly assiduous member. He said, "How's it going, Terry?" to the blind newsdealer on the corner and Terence Corrigan said, "Nothing to complain about, Nate." Shapiro bought a sports final and glanced at the headlines as he walked the last half block. "WELL-KNOWN PAINTER SUICIDE," he read. The headline was below the fold, but it was a two-column line. Shapiro was mildly surprised at the descriptive words.

When Nathan Shapiro opened his apartment door he knew they were having a goulash for dinner—the special goulash, made to Rose's grandmother's recipe. He knew Rose had walked the dog because the dog was on a forbidden sofa. She got down hurriedly when Shapiro went into the living room. She went under the sofa.

Rose came in from the kitchen and said, "Another long day, darling," and he bent down to kiss her. He had to bend some way down because Rose Shapiro was a small woman–a small, dark woman, neatly made. It occurred to Shapiro that if he had to write a description of his wife for circulation to other policemen (which he would never need to do), he would use almost the same words he would use if he described Myra Dedek. "Five feet four." That would do for either of them. "Black hair, dark brown eyes." That described them both. "Weight: 115." Perhaps "118" would be more accurate for Rose Shapiro, but one does not weigh people with one's eyes. Nor, actually, does one describe them with one's words.

"Tight mouth." That would do for Myra Dedek. It would not for Rose, whose mouth was tender, full-lipped. There were laughter crinkles at the corners of Rose Shapiro's eyes. Myra Dedek's face looked as if it had been freshly ironed. Rose's soft black hair was short and it seemed to fluff of its own accord. Probably she had just washed it under the shower. She would, Shapiro thought, look better than Myra Dedek did in a perfectly cut blue silk suit. But they did not run to suits like that on what a policeman made, even when the policeman had, by some fluke, been promoted to lieutenant. Even when a policeman's wife teaches school.

"Same woman," Rose said. "I know you're late, but it hasn't been that long. So that you'd forget what I looked like. Sit down and take your shoes off."

He sat down, but did not take his shoes off. He did take off his suit jacket and unstrap the shoulder holster, which his gun made heavy. Rose took the holstered revolver and put it on the shelf where it lived when it did not live against the lean chest of Nathan Shapiro, detective lieutenant assigned to Homicide, South.

She brought him a stemmed glass of rather sweet red wine, which was all his stomach would withstand. She made herself a martini, and rubbed a twisted lemon peel around the edge of the chilled glass. They sat side by side on a sofa which faced the small, non-wood-burning–non-anything burning, except electricity–fireplace. Above the fireplace was a portrait, in oil, of Shapiro's father, Rabbi Emmanuel Shapiro.

"That," Nathan Shapiro said, and raised his glass to the portrait of his father, "is representational."

"That is Papa," Rose said. "And very like him, darling. The skullcap's not quite straight, but anybody'd know it's Papa. You've been looking at it seven years."

Shapiro continued to look at the portrait. The painter had signed it; signed it in the lower right-hand corner. The signature was clear and precise. "I. Blum."

"Would you say Isaac Blum was a good painter?" Shapiro asked his wife.

She shrugged her shoulders slightly. Then she shook her head.

"No, I don't suppose I would," Rose Shapiro said. She looked at the portrait and shook her head again. "It looks like Papa," she said. "The eyes are like his were. Good eyes, weren't they, Nathan?"

"He was a good man," Nathan Shapiro said.

"That," Rose said. "Certainly that. More than that, of course. A scholar. A learned man. Without being at all a *'shiva bucha.*"

Not a "dimple-fingers." Not a Jewish scholar whose soft hands touch nothing more harsh than pages of the Talmud, than ancient books and manuscripts of exegeses.

"An intelligent man," Rose added. "A man who served. Isaac Blum painted his portrait because he loved him, Nathan. Looked up to him. It was Isaac's way of showing that. Does it matter that he wasn't really a good painter?"

Nathan Shapiro shook his head. He continued to look at the painting of Rabbi Emmanuel Shapiro, who had been a scholar and a man of quick and subtle mind. And a man to be loved by those of his congregation, including Isaac Blum, who had been a cutter by trade and worked on Seventh Avenue. Shapiro sighed and thought, like father unlike son. A son who is really good only with a gun.

"You're like him, you know," Rose told her husband, knowing he would not believe her. "Drink your wine, darling. The goulash will dry out."

It is preposterous for her to say I am like my father, Nathan Shapiro thought. It is gentle and tolerant of her, but absurd.

She knows better, of course. After many years of knowing me she can not help knowing better.

"Why?" Rose said. She did not need to explain the question.

"I've spent most of the afternoon looking at pictures," her husband told her. "Very different. Not very comprehensible."

"Because of Mr. Jones?" Rose said. She had, Nathan Shapiro thought, bought a newspaper while she was walking the dog. The dog, a Scotty bitch named Cleo, had come out from under the sofa and gone to lie on a chair, which also was forbidden her. She knew when people were not in a frame of mind to notice dogs.

"Bill Weigand handed it to me," Shapiro told his wife. "Nobody else free, I guess. I'm making a muddle of it, as he ought to have known I would."

"Of course you are, darling," Rose said, and looked at him fondly—a little hopelessly, but fondly. "Abstract, these paintings you've been looking at?"

He nodded his head, dimly.

"No wonder you're tired," Rose said. "Finish your wine and we'll eat." She smiled at him. "While the goulash is still representational."

Captain William Weigand, commanding, Homicide, South, finished reading the typed report on the desk in front of him and looked across the desk at the sad-faced man who sat opposite.

"Not much, is it?" Shapiro said, with the intention of saying it first. "I'm out of my depth, Bill. Not the sort of thing I'm any good at. Johnny Stein, now."

"No," Weigand said. "It's your baby, Nate. A slippery baby apparently. But yours to cuddle. You agree with the M.E.'s man? Right?"

"Yes," Shapiro said. "I'd call it homicide. As much hunch as anything."

"Then it's ours," Weigand told him. "Because of the angle of the shot? And that he'd apparently planned to have a guest for dinner? Or supper? Hot bird and cold bottle. And . . . ?"

"Perfectly healthy, according to the autopsy," Shapiro said.

"So we can count that out. He looked as healthy as a dead man can. Mrs. Dedek says his work was falling off, but this man Briskie says it wasn't. It's all there, Bill." He pointed to the report which was the "there."

"Mrs. Dedek says she wasn't going to help him eat the squabs and drink the champagne. This girl Rachel Farmer says she wasn't. And Mrs. Briskie–" he consulted the typed sheet in front of him– "knew him only casually. Had never been to his apartment. Can't imagine where you got the idea she might have been planning to have dinner with him. Or supper. You didn't tell her about the Farmer girl's insinuation?"

"No."

"Right. Who his guest was to have been probably hasn't anything to do with it, anyway."

"A loose end of string," Shapiro said. "Something to pull at. But probably you're right. Johnny Stein, now ——"

"No, Nate," Weigand said. "The baby's yours."

It was worth one more try, and Nathan Shapiro gave it one more try. He knew nothing about the kind of people who were involved–painters, models, song writers. People who ran art galleries. People who didn't seem to know, or care, whether or not they had any clothes on. People who painted pictures that didn't mean anything and made sketches of women with two faces from models who had only one.

"I'll never understand any of it," Shapiro said. "Take this one thing, Bill. One person who ought to know says Jones was painted out. Another, who's in the same line, says he was getting better, not worse. Maybe it isn't important. I don't know. And I don't know which one is lying. Damn it all, I've no way of knowing. They all look alike to me. The pictures, I mean. None of them makes any sense."

"Wouldn't to me," Weigand said. "And wouldn't to Johnny Stein either, Nate."

"I'm not trying to dodge a job. It's just that I . . ."

He was told not to be a damn fool. He was told that nobody thought he was trying to dodge a job. With that, Weigand looked over Shapiro's head, at nothing in particular.

"We get off course on something," Weigand said, still addressing the opposite wall, or himself. "We look around for a pilot. Right? Toxicologist, maybe. Psychiatrist sometimes. Or a man who knows about wood. Or automobile mechanics. Have to go outside the department for some of them. Right, Nate?"

Nathan Shapiro sighed and nodded his agreement.

"Somebody who knows something about modern art, this time," Weigand said. "Somebody we can trust."

"It would help," Shapiro said. "God knows it would help."

"You haven't met my wife, have you?" Weigand asked him.

"No."

"You're going to," Weigand said. He reached for the telephone.

Detective Anthony Cook stopped the car in front of a tall and shining apartment house on the upper East Side. He said, "Jeeze. The captain must be in the chips. Hate to think what they nick you in a place like this."

Cook was new to Homicide, South; he was new to Manhattan and to the Detective Division. He probably, Shapiro thought, getting out of the police car, wonders if Weigand has had his hand out somewhere along the line. There had been cops who had held hands out, in the long history of the New York Police Department.

"Got money of his own," Shapiro said, telling Cook what was generally known in the department. "Somebody left him money years ago, when he was already on the cops. Pounding a beat like anybody. Way you did. Way I did. He stayed on the cops."

"Why the hell?"

"I don't know, Tony," Shapiro said. "Ask him some time if you want to. Maybe he'll tell you. Maybe he'll just wonder why you need to ask."

Tony Cook said, "Uh," and said it thoughtfully. He drove off on his errand, which was to return to Mrs. Myra Dedek the notarized document that, on its face, gave her unrestricted right to sell the paintings of Shackleford Jones, deceased. Shapiro went into the lobby of the apartment house, and to the desk where a young man in uniform stood. The young man smiled with marked detachment in the general direction of the long-faced detective. He said, "Can I help you, sir?"

"Mrs. Weigand," Shapiro said, and was asked who he should say, sir? Shapiro told him who to say and that he was expected. The attendant said, "Certainly, sir," his voice as detached as his smile. He used a desk telephone. He said, "A Mr. Shapiro, Mrs. Weigand. A Mr. Nathan Shapiro." He listened momentarily. He said, "Certainly, Mrs. Weigand," and cradled the phone and said, "Eighteen C, Lieutenant. The elevator's on your left."

Shapiro pressed a button beside a door marked "18 C" and chimes sounded beyond it. At the first note, the door opened.

She wore dark green slacks and a white blouse and a jacket which matched the slacks. She was slim and her brown hair had a hint of red in it and her eyes were green. Perhaps, Shapiro thought, looking down at her, the green in her eyes was a color borrowed from slacks and jacket. Probably, in another light, in a different costume, her eyes would be another color. Gray, perhaps. Or even hazel.

"Yes," Dorian Weigand said, "they're really green, Lieutenant. Come in."

She turned with that and he followed her into a big room. The far wall of the room was glass and sunlight came through it and lay bright on a deep yellow carpet.

There was a flowing grace in Dorian Weigand's movement as she walked through the big room toward the glass wall with which it ended. She moved, Shapiro thought, as a cat moves. And he thought, There is nothing planned about her moving so. ("Ht. 5–7; wt. 115.")

There was a long, low table in front of the glass wall of the room, and a sketch pad was lying on it, face down.

"Sit there and you can see the river," Dorian said, and indicated a chair, not in the sunlight, which faced the enormous window. Beyond the glass, far below, was the East River. A tug was towing a lumbering barge up it, toward Hell Gate.

Dorian Weigand sat in a deep chair facing the one she had pointed out to Nathan Shapiro. She seemed to flow into the chair, and one of her long legs curled into it, under the other. She said, "Now," and waited, without seeming to wait.

Shapiro had been briefed by the husband of this green-eyed woman.

"Used to do fashion sketches," Bill Weigand had said, after he had used the telephone on his desk and ended by saying, "I hope I can, darling. Let you know later."

Shapiro had had no trouble in guessing the question Bill Weigand answered. He had answered with much the same words, often enough. "Can you make it home to dinner?" That had been the question. It is one often asked by the wives of policemen.

". . . fashion sketches. Still does, now and then, but she's not tied down to it. Mostly, now, she does cartoons. Magazines use a good many of them. Does a few for what they call 'institutional ads.' She signs them, 'Hunt.' That was her maiden name. Does watercolors, too. Doesn't show them. Has shown her cartoons a few times. And she likes to go and look at pictures, Nate. All kinds of pictures. She's bought a few."

Sitting where he could look down at the East River, Nathan Shapiro remembered that, and looked at the walls which were not glass. Over a fireplace–which would burn wood, and evidently had–there was a large framed painting, done in greens and yellows. It seemed to change as he looked at it. For a moment it was merely shapes and colors. Then it was, almost clearly, yellow flowers in green vases.

"The Captain said you might be willing to help me, Mrs. Weigand," Shapiro said. "There's this case I've fallen heir to. Bill's–I mean the Captain's–assigned me —"

"I," Dorian said, "call him Bill too, Lieutenant. So it wasn't suicide. You and Bill think somebody murdered Shack Jones."

She did not phrase it as a question, but Shapiro answered it as one. He said, "I think so, Mrs. Weigand. All your husband has to go on is what I dig up." He sighed. "Could be I'm wrong. Could be I'm messing things up." He sighed again, and Dorian Weigand looked at him with interest. She saw a long-faced man with a long, straight nose and deeply brown eyes. He looks sad, she thought; looks sad and without confidence. But he is a lieutenant, and not old for it and advancement in rank is not normally rapid in the Police Department of the City of New York. And Bill has given him this case. Bill must think more highly of this sad-faced man than this man thinks of himself.

"What it comes to," Shapiro said, "I don't know anything about art, Mrs. Weigand. What it means. What it's all about." And then, unexpectedly, he smiled and that changed his face. "Don't even know what I like," he said.

" 'Guide through the world of art,' " Dorian said, quoting what Bill had said on the telephone–said lightly, amusement at his own phrasing underlying his words. "I'll do what I can, of course. But I'm not really in the world of art, Lieutenant. Not really in the world at all. It won't have me. I'm commercial. They draw the line sharply."

Shapiro shook his head.

"Men like Mr. Jones sell their paintings," he said. "You do cartoons, Bill tells me, and sell them."

"Sometimes on assignment," she said. "One of the differences. And an illustrator is one thing. A serious artist is another. And never the twain shall meet. Only they do. Sometimes in the same man, come to that."

"Shackleford Jones?"

"Never an illustrator, so far as I know," Dorian said. "All serious artist. They pre-empt that word, you know–'artist.' A writer is a writer. A composer is a composer. An architect is an architect, even if he's Frank Lloyd Wright. A photographer is a photographer, even if he's Steichen. A painter is an artist. Period. Even if he isn't."

"Jones was? Good, I mean? That may come into it, Mrs. Weigand. Not that I know what comes into it. Or that anything does. It's still possible that he killed himself. Precinct thinks so and they were there first."

She is easy to talk to, this green-eyed wife of Bill Weigand's, Shapiro thought. She's making herself easy to talk to, I suppose because I'm not.

"Shack Jones had a name," Dorian said. "Or was getting one.

I don't really know his work, Nathan. The Dedek Galleries has two, on more or less permanent exhibit. I've seen those."

"You liked them?"

She thought for a moment.

"Yes," she said. "I think so. I'm not sure I'd want to live with them. But, yes, I think they are good paintings. It may be, of course, that Myra picked his best. She–or he–set the prices high enough, heaven knows. Which is probably why the exhibit has turned out to be so permanent. They were there a year ago, when Myra gave me a share of a group show of cartoons. Although 'gave' isn't precisely the word. We paid for the ads. *And* the programs. And she took her forty per cent."

"Forty?"

"She wanted fifty," Dorian said. "I–haggled her down." She laughed, then. She had a quick, gay laugh. "I still wasn't very commercial," Dorian Weigand said. "None of the department stores made me offers. There wasn't any rush of private collectors, either."

Shapiro said, "Department stores?"

"That's rather recent," Dorian said. "Department stores and Fifth Avenue shops have discovered art, more or less all at once. Gives painters a new outlet. Of course, a good many of them scream their heads off and talk about prostitution. But a good many of them, particularly the ones coming up, go along. Painters, too, have to buy groceries. The stores pay cash."

Shapiro said he hadn't known about that. He added that he didn't know about any of this.

"Some of the stores," she told him, "have set up galleries. Usually in connection with their furniture departments, if they have them. They buy paintings outright, for low prices and directly from the painters. They add their markup, just as they do on the dresses they buy on Seventh Avenue. As they do on all the commodities they sell. Some of the paintings are quite good and a few are very good, and most of them, I suppose, are botches. But the same thing goes for most commodities, doesn't it? For dresses and fabrics and beds and tables?"

The world of Fifth Avenue shops was an alien world to

Shapiro, a world almost as alien as the "world of art" through which, bemused, he wandered now. Rose bought her clothes from stores in Brooklyn. To Nathan Shapiro's eyes they looked fine on her.

"Would a man like Mr. Jones sell paintings to the stores?"

She did not really know. Possibly, if he needed money. He would not, certainly, get anything like the prices he asked for the canvases on exhibition in the Dedek Galleries. But he apparently did not get them there, either.

"He had a name of sorts," Dorian said. "As 'Shack.' At a guess, he wouldn't."

But that was only a guess. He was very modern; very abstract. The stores, for the most part, did not put so much of a strain on prospective customers. And the stores paid, for the most part, in hundreds. Shackleford Jones apparently thought in thousands.

She had had dealings with Myra Dedek. What could she tell him about Mrs. Dedek?

She was a widow. Her husband had been Anton Dedek, an importer. Apparently a successful one. Myra had started her gallery after her husband died, it was generally assumed on the money he had left her. She had a reputation–a reputation for sharpness and shrewdness. "Some people think 'ruthless' is the word." Hers was a good gallery. "In."

"She says she advanced money to Jones. A considerable amount, she says. Over a period of years."

That was not unprecedented. Dealers did, sometimes, tide over painters they thought good, likely to sell.

"For the most part," Dorian said, "painters need a bit of tiding over. A good many people buy paintings nowadays. That's 'in', too. But there are a good many painters."

"Mrs. Dedek," Shapiro said, "thinks that Jones's work had fallen off in the last few years. That he was painted out. Offers that as a reason for suicide. Does that seem likely to you?"

"I can't," Dorian said, "think of any likely reason for suicide. I don't know what kind of man Mr. Jones was. If you devote your life to something and it falls out from under you. . . ." She ended that by lifting her shoulders.

"A man I've talked to," Shapiro said. "He's an artist–painter–too, says that Jones's work was getting better, not worse. I don't know whether this man–a man named Briskie–knows what he's talking about. The trouble is that I don't know whether any of these people know what they're talking about. Did you ever hear of a painter named Briskie, Mrs. Weigand?"

"I don't think–" Dorian said, and stopped with that. She looked at nothing for a moment and then said, "Wait." Shapiro waited.

"I don't know his work," Dorian said. "Or whether he knows what he's talking about. But the name–it's not a common name. Is it Maxwell Briskie?"

"Yes."

"He's married to a composer," Dorian said. "A woman who writes under the name Dorothy Goodbody. Is that the man?"

"Yes," Shapiro said. "That's the man, Mrs. Weigand. He says that, during the last two or three years, Jones was almost as good as he thought he was. You see the point, Mrs. Weigand."

"Whether Myra is providing a motive for suicide by making one up. Yes."

Her tone was not tolerant. But Shapiro sighed, lamenting himself. Only a stupidly groping man asks an intelligent woman if she has seen an obvious point.

"I'm sorry," Shapiro said.

She laughed lightly. She said there was nothing to be sorry about.

"Of course," Shapiro said, "he may have had another reason to kill himself. We may come on it. Meanwhile. . . ." He shrugged, this time.

"Meanwhile," Dorian said, "confirmation or rejection of Myra's theory. Why would she? Unless ––"

"Conceivably," Shapiro said, "she has a good deal of his early work on hand. Wants to spread the word that his recent paintings are inferior."

"Conceivably." She did not sound especially convinced. "Did he date his paintings, do you know? Some of them do and some don't."

Shapiro did not know.

“I’m not an expert,” she said. “Certainly not a critic. Did Bill suggest I am?”

“You’ll have opinions. Informed. Mine aren’t, you see. I’m over my head.” He paused and looked down at the East River. The tug was still huffing its barge toward Hell Gate. Against the tide, probably, Shapiro thought.

“My wife and I,” Shapiro said, “have a painting in our apartment. A portrait of my father. He was a rabbi. I’ve been looking at it for years and thinking–oh, that it was a pretty good picture of my father. Looked a good deal as he looked. Last night I really looked at it.”

“Yes,” Dorian said. “Things happen that way. Shack’s studio is downtown, isn’t it?”

“West Village. In something called Little Great Smith Street. I could have a car sent over.”

“We can use mine,” she said, and got up and walked toward a telephone–flowed toward a telephone and used it to ask a man named George to have her car brought around.

“Let’s hope he did date them,” Dorian said. “It’ll only take me minutes to change. I can’t go around outside in slacks.”

Shapiro thought she could–and very well, too. But he did not say so. It was none of his business.

VI

He must remember, she told him, driving a big Buick expertly down Fifth Avenue, that she could only give him an opinion. Actually, the opinion would be no better than his own. Essentially no better.

"It's something you understand," Shapiro said. "Something I don't at all. I told you, I don't even know what I like."

"Or," she said, "haven't confidence. Oh, I've seen a good many –you intolerable bully!" The last was to a bus which had turned into her path without signaling any such intention. "Pictures. I like to look at them. Some I like a great deal and some only a little and a great many not at all. It's just–I don't know what it is. Oh, you can explain it, one way or the other, to yourself afterward. But that's after the fact, not the fact itself."

"There aren't standards?"

"Those are after the fact, too. Oh, daubs. Daubs are another matter. A man can't draw, and that's that. Can't use color, and that's that. Of course, intentional distortion–that's another matter, too. And not everybody sees colors the same ——" She blasted on the Buick's horn to interrupt herself. A young man with very long hair had walked in front of the car, and against the lights. Instead of jumping at the horn's warning, he slowed his already sauntering pace to glare at Dorian Weigand and Nathan Shapiro.

"Perhaps," Dorian said, "he's thinking himself a poem."

"Or," Shapiro said, "where his next fix is coming from. We may as well go through Ninth Street, Mrs. Weigand."

"Policemen," Dorian said, but the derision in her tone was entirely friendly. "Always thinking the worst of people."

She turned the Buick into Ninth Street toward Sixth.

"I almost wouldn't marry Bill because he was a policeman," she said. "Because it was his job to hunt people down. That was quite a while ago, of course. I was–it doesn't matter."

Lights stopped them at Sixth Avenue. Lights released them into Christopher Street. Shapiro gave directions, then hoping–but doubting–that they would prove accurate. They got the Buick to Little Great Smith Street. It was hot in the studio.

"Bad for his paintings," Dorian said. "Pigments–canvases too, for that matter–like an equable climate. He probably couldn't afford air conditioning. Although a good many painters —"

"He could," Shapiro told her, and found air conditioners–one in a window at the end of the room; another, larger, let into a wall. He turned them on and the room began to hum.

Dorian went from easel to easel.

"This one isn't finished," she said of one. "Was he working on it when he was killed, do you know?"

Shapiro did not know. If she meant at the precise moment he was shot, he thought not. "Apparently on this," he said, and walked to the easel to which Jones had thumbtacked drawing paper on which to sketch an attenuated woman (or plucked ostrich). Dorian looked at the sketch for some seconds. Then she nodded. "He could draw," she said. "What I meant by intentional distortion." She nodded again. "Could have been a good fashion artist," she said. "Women impossibly long and skinny. Of course, they would need to have clothes on."

"Is this one finished?"

That, she said, probably depended on how far he had planned to go with it. It might be a preliminary sketch for a painting, a way of fixing a composition in his mind. In that case, he might have finished with it.

She was standing in the chalked outline of a body. She looked down at it and at the floor around it and stepped out of the outline.

She stopped again in front of the unfinished painting. She went around the studio, looking at paintings displayed on easels, sliding paintings on stretchers out of racks. At some she looked for minutes; at others she seemed hardly to look at all. She took two canvases of approximately the same size out of a rack and propped them side by side against the wall and looked from one to the other.

"He did date them," she said, without turning from the paintings. "Most of them, anyway. These two are four years apart. The more recent this year."

"And . . . ?"

She turned from the paintings. She said, "Myra Dedek is a professional, Nathan. It is her business to know paintings. I'm a cartoonist and when I run out of ideas I do small watercolors. Mostly pictures of what I can see out of the apartment windows. I was doing the barge when the desk called to say you were downstairs. A barge inching against the tide. Trying to get some feeling of the tug's effort. Getting nowhere with it. Not my métier, painting isn't. I told you that."

"But . . . ?"

"Say I don't agree with Myra," Dorian Weigand said. "I think he was painting better this year than he painted four years ago. And don't ask me why I think that. Do you ever read art criticism? Or music criticism, for that matter?"

"No."

"Mostly," she said, "the words they use don't really fit what they are writing about. Or it seems to me they don't. Words are about concepts–about emotions, ideas. Paintings–paintings are just *there*. When you try to talk about them, and it's the same when you try to write about them, you–oh, make up allegories. And try to impale the intangible on word spikes."

She was, Shapiro thought, talking at least partly to herself. Her precise meaning floated a little beyond his reach. But so many things did.

"Bill," Dorian said, "gets hunches. Perhaps that's partly what I'm trying to say." She looked at Shapiro intently. "I think you do, too," she said. "Things look a certain way, but you don't accept that way. Or–do accept it. Not because you can prove or disprove it. Wait —"

He waited.

"I've read the stories about this case. It looked like suicide, didn't it? You can't prove it wasn't, can you? But you have a hunch it wasn't. And you try to back up your hunch?"

"It comes to that, sometimes."

"I like this one," she said, and pointed to one of the canvases. "I like it better than the one he painted four years ago. Much better. So, I can say it's stronger than the other. Or more alive than the other. Or that the composition is more assured. And all I'm saying is that I like it better. Somebody else might not."

"There wouldn't be general agreement? Among people who know about things like this?"

For a moment, then, she closed her green eyes, and drew her eyebrows a little together, so that vertical lines formed on her forehead. She opened her eyes.

"Yes," she said. "I think there would be, Nathan. I think most people who are interested in painting, and who have seen a good many paintings, would agree with me. That Shack was a good painter and getting to be a better one. Working out a style which was only *his* style." She smiled suddenly. "That's my hunch, Nathan," she said. "For what it's —"

She broke off, and Shapiro, who had heard it too, turned with her to face the door to the studio, in the lock of which somebody had just turned a key. Rachel Farmer coming back to have another try at studio-lifting?

The woman who came through the door she had opened with one of Shackleford Jones's widely distributed keys was as unlike Rachel Farmer as a woman could well be. She was short, almost dumpy, and she took little steps into the big room and looked around it like an uncertain bird. Her hair was a somewhat unconvincing auburn and was very tightly curled. She had large blue eyes and she peered through them as if she needed glasses. She was well into the room before she saw the two who were looking at her. Then she said, "Oh!"

She stood for a moment and peered at them, and Shapiro thought that peering did not help her very much. She came on toward them until she was quite close. Then she said, "Hello," apparently to both of them, and stopped and looked up at Shapiro.

"If you're Mr. Osgood," she said, "how did you get in?"

"You expected a Mr. Osgood to meet you here?"

"Of course. It was all arranged. As soon as I heard, I got my lawyer to call a lawyer in New York and he said Mr. Osgood would be the man. So I sent Mr. Osgood a telegram and he wired back all right and said that the studio would be the best place if I had a key to it and of course I did and–are you somebody Mr. Osgood sent instead?"

On this one, Shapiro thought, everything seemed to begin in the middle.

"No," Shapiro said. "I'm not representing Mr. Osgood. He would be the man for what, Mrs. ——?" He gave her a chance to give a name. She did not seem to notice the chance.

"An expert, of course," the plump little woman–the woman who wore a flowered summer dress which was entirely wrong for her–said, as one who says the obvious to the backward. "An appraiser. He's famous."

"Jeremiah Osgood?" Dorian said.

The dumpy woman turned toward her and said, "Of course. Who are you?"

"My name is Weigand," Dorian said. "Dorian Weigand."

"I never heard of you. One way or another I heard of a lot of his girls, but never about anybody named Dorian. What are you doing here, anyway?"

With a glance and slightly raised eyebrows, Dorian passed it to Nathan Shapiro.

"Helping me," Shapiro said. "I'm Lieutenant Shapiro of ——"

"You don't look like a lieutenant to me," the woman said. "And I've got a nephew in the Air Force. He's a *captain.*"

"Not that kind of lieutenant," Shapiro said. "Police lieutenant, Mrs. ——?" She was "missis" from the ring on her left hand. Her finger had swollen into the ring.

"Who do you think?" she said. "His wife, of course. Who would I be?"

"Shackleford Jones's wife?"

"For twenty years. Of course, I was very young when we were married. Barely sixteen."

Shapiro a little doubted that, but his doubt was one which did not matter. He looked down at her. She must, he thought, have been pretty twenty years ago–twenty years and a good many pounds ago. That did not matter either, probably.

"You came here to have Mr. Osgood appraise your husband's pictures. I take it you don't live in New York?"

"I should say not. Two years of that was enough. And down here in what they call the Village, too. Riffraff. And from what I saw coming here in a cab it's even worse now. A disgrace to America, that's what it is."

"Where do you live, Mrs. Jones," Shapiro asked, and rather expected that "God's country" would be the answer. It was not.

"Kansas," Mrs. Shackleford Jones said, with righteous emphasis. "Emporia, Kansas. Born there and brought up there."

"Did you meet Mr. Jones there? Was he born and brought up there, too?"

"Kansas City. The Missouri side. And it really oughtn't to be called *Kansas* City at all. And in some ways it's almost as bad as New York. Saloons and gangsters and . . ."

Dorian had wandered deeper into the studio and was looking at more pictures. But she was, evidently, still within earshot of Mrs. Jones's notably carrying voice. Dorian, just audibly, hummed a few bars from *Oklahoma!* "Everything is up to date in Kansas City," were the words which went with the tune.

"You met him there, Mrs. Jones? What's your given name, by the way?"

"Isabelle, if it makes any difference. No, he was on the road for his father."

"On the road?"

"Taking orders. Learning the business. And —"

"Orders for what, Mrs. Jones?"

"Groceries, of course. His father was Jones and Hartnett. He was wholesale. And every two weeks or so he–I mean Shackleford, of course–would come around and take orders from Daddy."

"Your father is in the grocery business?"

"Of course. He has a beautiful store. Cronin, Food Specialities. Better than Wolferman's in Kansas City, everybody thinks. Maybe not as big but ——" She stopped suddenly. "Why are you asking all these questions?" she asked Nathan Shapiro, who was not sure of an answer which would be adequate to her or, for that matter, to himself.

"Your husband died violently, Mrs. Jones," Shapiro said. "When that happens, it always brings the police in."

"Committed suicide, it said on the radio. And I wasn't really surprised, living the way he did."

"When did you hear the news, Mrs. Jones?"

She had heard it the afternoon of the day before–Thursday. She had got a local flight out of Emporia to Kansas City; a nonstop flight to New York, and made it all–apparently including telephone calls and telegrams–by midevening at Kennedy International. She had been, Shapiro thought, brisk about it.

"Whatever he left is mine, isn't it? That's the law. Not that I suppose all this–" she encompassed the big studio with a gesture of a pudgy hand–"is worth anything much. But Daddy said there wouldn't be any harm in finding out. He said he'd read in the *Star* that sometimes people paid crazy prices for pictures. *Pictures!*"

"So you decided to get an expert–this Mr. Osgood–to appraise your late husband's paintings?"

"Make an inventory," she said. She looked around the studio, but made no movement to walk around it. "Probably a waste of time and money," she said. "Anybody can see that. A lot of rubbish. And I told him, if he thought he had to draw pictures, one of the biggest card companies in the world was in Kansas City, and that somebody had to do their pictures."

"Card companies?"

"Greeting cards. Mother's Day and Christmas. And little poems on most of them. And the pictures are sweet–really sweet. But he said, 'My God, Belle–' he called me Belle–as if I'd said something silly. But really, I guess, he knew he wasn't good enough to do pictures like they wanted."

"Probably that was it," Shapiro said, and heard movement

from the rear of the studio—movement and a small voice sound, which he did not attempt to characterize.

Dorian walked toward them, and walked briskly, as if she had suddenly remembered an appointment.

"I'm more convinced than ever about what we were talking about," she said. "But you want to talk to Mrs. Jones, of course. And I'm really supposed to meet some friends for lunch." She had moved so the short, plump woman was between them. And over Mrs. Jones's curly head Dorian Weigand just perceptibly winked at Nathan Shapiro.

She said, "Good-bye, Mrs. Jones," and walked to the door. At the door she turned back. "There's a picture back there," she said. "In the second rack from the windows. Quite representational. It has a catalogue number on it, Nathan. Seventy-nine. I'm not at all sure, but I think it might interest you."

She opened the door and stepped into the doorway, but then turned back again.

"I'll be home by two," she said. "If you want to telephone me, Lieutenant."

"She's got a nerve," Mrs. Shackleford Jones said, her voice pitched to carry, Shapiro suspected, to the ears of Dorian Weigand, who was just closing the door behind her. The door closed behind Dorian with a perceptible snap. "Rummaging around here," Annabelle Jones said, "as if she had a right. These —these *things* Shackleford did are mine, aren't they? Whether they're worth anything or not?"

"Do you know if your husband left a will, Mrs. Jones? Leaving his pictures to you?"

"What difference does that make? I'm his wife. I can prove I'm his wife."

Shapiro said he was sure she could. And asked again whether she knew if her husband had left a will.

"It would be like him not to," she said. "He never did anything like that right. He was scatterbrained."

"As his wife," Shapiro said, "you have dower rights—not less than a third of whatever is realized. After taxes, of course. And after payment of whatever legal debts he may have left. And,

I'd suppose, any contractual obligations he may have taken on. I'm not a lawyer."

"What you're saying is, somebody is going to try to cheat me out of what's mine."

"No. Only that there may be issues for the courts to decide. If a will isn't turned up, the courts will appoint an executor, probably. And he will order an appraisal." He looked down at the plump little woman. The vagueness, he thought, had gone out of her large, watery blue eyes.

"They won't accept what this Mr. Osgood tells them? If he ever shows up?"

"If he's qualified as an expert," Shapiro told her. "But the courts probably will want someone demonstrably impartial. Not somebody you have employed."

"I'll get a lawyer. I'll see about this. I know how you people are here in New York. Daddy warned ——"

The ringing of a telephone cut through her words. The telephone was deep in the studio and Shapiro zigzagged between easels to it. He said, "Hello," and was asked by a crisply speaking woman whether a Mrs. Jones was there. The voice added that Mr. Osgood had been trying to reach her at the Hilton because he had had to make a change ——

"Yes," Shapiro said. "Mrs. Jones is here. Expecting Mr. Osgood." He put a hand over the transmitter and looked up the length of the studio and took in breath to call. He let the breath out again. Mrs. Isabelle Jones was closing the studio door firmly behind her.

"Mrs. Jones seems to have left," Shapiro told whoever was calling in behalf of Mr. Jeremiah Osgood. Then he added a question: "She is registered at the Hilton?"

"Oh, yes. She merely wasn't–to whom am I talking?"

The voice had suddenly become as guarded as the grammar.

"A police lieutenant," Shapiro said, and got a startled "Oh," and then, "I'd better ——"

"This is Mr. Jeremiah Osgood," a male voice said. "You say you're from the police?"

It was evident that Osgood had been listening on an extension.

"Lieutenant Nathan Shapiro." Then, after a momentary pause, "Homicide."

"It seems," Mr. Jeremiah Osgood said, "that my attorney was correct in advising me against premature entanglement. In warning me of possible litigation."

His voice was as carefully cultured as his phrasing was elaborately unreal.

"You called to tell Mrs. Jones you've decided to back out?" Shapiro asked Jeremiah Osgood. "That was the idea?"

He could hear Osgood draw in his breath, possibly in recoil against crudity.

"For the moment," Osgood said. "That is a correct assumption, Lieutenant. In my position in the art world ——"

Shapiro cut through that.

"You know Jones's work, Mr. Osgood?"

"Certainly. Most assuredly."

"Is it good?"

"In my opinion," Osgood said, "it, at its best, achieves a degree of imponderable permanence."

Shapiro said, "Thanks," and hung up. He used the telephone to call in, and got Anthony Cook, who had found Myra Dedek at her gallery–which was quite a place–and given her the agreement signed by the late Shackleford Jones and got back the receipt.

"There's a Mrs. Shackleford Jones at the Hilton," Shapiro told him. "Says she's the widow. Says she lives in something called Emporia, Kansas. Says she left there by plane yesterday afternoon after she heard on the radio her husband was dead. I'm at Jones's studio and she was. All at once she hightailed it out."

"Bring her in?"

Shapiro considered for a moment.

"Check her out in this Emporia," he said. "Her father apparently owns a grocery store. Name's Cronin, apparently. Ask the Emporia boys to check on when she did fly out of there.

If she did fly out of there. If it jibes, just ask her to stay put in the hotel until we get a chance to talk to her. If she makes a fuss–she probably will–talk about the D.A.'s office and a formal statement. But not unless we have to."

Cook said, "O.K., Lieutenant."

"And," Shapiro said, "if one of the boys is sitting on his hands, have him check out a man named Jeremiah Osgood. Art dealer and expert, apparently. Makes a point of being *Mister* Osgood."

"Anything special about him?"

"Not at the moment. Reputation. General feel of the guy. Just in case. Mrs. Jones hired him–thought she'd hired him, anyway –to appraise her late husband's paintings. Which she expects to inherit. Although she thinks they're rubbish. Says she does. This expert Osgood, on the other hand, says they achieve a degree of imponderable permanence."

"Is that supposed to mean something?"

"I haven't the faintest idea," Nathan Shapiro said, and hung up and went to find a picture with the number "79" on it.

It took him a little time to find it. He had to pull several canvases from a grooved rack. When he found it, he found it large. He pulled it to a light.

The painting was entirely realistic–a little startlingly so to Nathan Shapiro. It was of a naked woman; a most luxuriant woman. She was half sitting, half lying on a sofa–a sofa upholstered in a striped fabric of deep yellow and soft white.

Shapiro had seen Mrs. Maxwell Briskie, professionally known as Dorothy Goodbody, only with clothes on, so he could not be certain how accurately Jones had painted her curving body. But he had been meticulously exact in the painting of her face.

He had been exact, also, in painting the fabric against which, so enticingly, she half reclined. Shapiro knew precisely where a sofa so upholstered could be found. He had, in fact, recently sat on it.

He caught Cook at the office just as Cook was leaving it. He told Cook where he would be during the next hour or so and, briefly, why.

VII

THE TELEPHONE WAS ringing when Dorian went into her apartment. She walked to it quickly—Bill might be calling; the sad, long-faced lieutenant might be calling; the bell might be about to give up fruitless ringing. She said, "Hello" and got, in a secretarial voice, "Mrs. Weigand? Mrs. Fields is calling. One moment, please."

She waited several moments. The advertising manager of Bryant & Washburn usually had many things going at once. Dorian had a chance to wonder if Nathan Shapiro had made anything out of the painting which carried a gallery catalogue number "79" and whether she herself had made too much of it. After all, she had based a guess on a newspaper photograph and that had been risky. If she were right, exhibiting it had been—call it rude. If ——

"Dorian? Been trying to get you all morning."

"I was ——"

"Want you to do a spot for us," Ursula Fields said. One seldom finished a sentence directed toward Ursula Fields. Ursula did not wait out the hesitant. "Free?"

"If you don't want it yesterday, Ursula."

Ursula Fields was rather in the habit of wanting things yesterday. This time, however, and after a brief snort, she said "Monday."

"If it jells."

"Even Tuesday. I'm tied up for lunch."

One sorted Ursula Fields's words out and put them in order. "After it, then?"

"Time enough before. If you get the lead out, dearie."

"As soon as I can," Dorian promised and thought how like Ursula Ursula was.

The glass wall at the end of the living room called to her, as it always called. She walked to it and looked down at the East River. A tanker was working down it toward, she supposed, the sea. The anxious little tug had towed its barge out of sight; perhaps now was laboring through Hell Gate toward the Sound. Dorian picked up the watercolor she had been working on. The tug did show its effort. Hobby painting, Dorian Weigand thought, and tore the sheet in half and then in half again. Occupational therapy.

She had changed from the green slack suit into a summer dress of greenish gray. It would do very well for the advertising department of Bryant & Washburn. A new face was indicated; white gloves were required. She did the face and found clean gloves. She telephoned down a request that George do what he could to catch her a cab. The big Buick was nothing to try to park in Fifth Avenue. She followed her request to the lobby of the high apartment house. George had been lucky.

"Mrs. Fields is on the telephone," the receptionist told Dorian Weigand, in the Swedish modernity of Bryant & Washburn's eighth floor. (*Executive Offices Only.*) "She—just a moment, Mrs. Weigand."

Ursula Fields was large behind a large desk. She wore a gray suit and a white shirt and had straight, thick gray hair. And, as Dorian knew, was firmly, even devotedly, married and had two sons, one graduated that same month from the Columbia Law School and the other still at Yale.

"Our buyers turn up in the oddest places," Ursula Fields said. " 'Morning, dearie. Like it?"

"It's long," Dorian said. "Odd place to find a buyer?"

"Don't worry your head about the copy," Ursula Fields said. "What it is—buyer. Dressed like Bryant and Washburn. Maybe talking to cowboys. But—French cowboys. Berets? South of France. Horses. Chief thing is the pants, of course."

One sorted out. It was to be presumed that the horses were not wearing the pants.

"Want to do it? Your kind of thing, dearie. Funny as you want to, long as the pants show up. French cowboy pants. Casuals wants to do them for the gals. Eights and tens, I hope to God. Though I wouldn't put it past them to do some twelves."

"Just the spot? Elegant buyer and cowboys with pants on? I didn't know they had cowboys in the south of France."

"Neither did I, dearie. Still doesn't seem very likely. Yes, just the spot. Sally'll do the sketches of the little prancers. Nancy can give you a rough of the layout. O.K.?"

"It shoots a weekend. Bill and I had thought —"

"You and that Bill of yours. You're a pro, aren't you? We pay you enough, God knows."

The words of her own thought repeated themselves in Dorian's head. "Hobby painting." And Bill probably would be working over the weekend. "Homicide Squad, South. Captain William Weigand commanding." It had sounded good, once. It had, once, sounded like regular hours.

"I'll have a shot at it," Dorian said. "Signed, I suppose?"

"Part of what we pay for, dearie," Ursula Fields said. "Run along and talk to Nancy."

Dorian went along a corridor, and into a smaller office, and talked to Nancy Sperling, art director. She looked at a roughed layout–spot at the top, centered, using about a quarter of a newspaper page; squiggles occupying the rest, in lieu of the sketches of attenuated girls in French cowboy slacks which Sally Painter would supply. "With a little bit of inspiration," Nancy Sperling, who was slender and becomingly wore a black sheer from Better Dresses, fifth floor, told Dorian. "Convulse them, darling."

The executive elevator was, from its indicator, at the ground floor, presumably discharging executives for lunch. Dorian rode an escalator to the seventh floor, where one bank of customer elevators ended. Furniture. Fabrics. "The Decorators' Corner." "The Sleep Shop." "Desks, Traditional." The escalator landed her among sofas, also traditional. She walked among sofas toward a bank of elevators. There was a sign "Art Gallery" and the sign was shaped to point.

Dorian Weigand, by instinct, went as the sign directed.

The gallery opened from the floor of sofas and upholstered

chairs. There were pictures on the display-room walls, adding a homey touch to an acre or so of homeless overstuffed seats. Most of the pictures were in heavy gilt frames which distracted, but insufficiently, from the paintings themselves. Most of the paintings seemed to be portraits of men and women who had lived, stiffly and tepidly, a century or so ago. Briefly, Dorian Weigand wondered if customers bought portraits of simulated ancestors to go with sofas covered in restless monotones.

The gallery itself was somewhat different. It occupied several small rooms, one of them devoted to seascapes, all by one painter who, it appeared, lived within view of an extremely conventional sea—a sea full of large rocks on which waves obediently broke.

The room beyond was entirely different. Here "pop" and "op" competed. Here collage was noticeable and bristled out toward the observer in apparent anger. On one of them a spring—presumably from a large alarm clock—coiled as if to leap.

The next room again was different. Here the paintings, most of them not large, were modern in feeling. For the most part abstract but now and then, in their fashion, representational. One, and in front of it Dorian stood for several minutes, pictured a village street which pitched sharply down toward, she thought, a river. Houses and store buildings clung precariously to the precipitous street. The picture had a title: "Foster, Missouri." It had a price: $275. It had been painted—Dorian leaned close to the canvas—by a man whose name appeared to be Sanders. "San" something, at any rate. Dorian put "San-something" in her mind for reference. She thought somebody could get himself a bargain for two hundred and seventy-five dollars.

She moved on along the wall and did not, for a good many pictures, hesitate again. Most of those she passed had, she thought, been passed often. On some the slips of paper which served as price tags had yellowed with their waiting; one or two had begun to curl away from the frames to which they were pasted. None of the neglected canvases was, Dorian thought, really bad. But none of them was especially good. Spots of color for walls which needed spots of color; unassertive pictures with which one could live untroubled and unconcerned.

She should, Dorian thought, go home and get her own sketch pad and get about her own work—get about a sketch of a buyer for Bryant & Washburn looking, with inspiration dawning in her eyes, at French cowboys in very special pants. She should, at least, go home—go somewhere—and have lunch. She had told Nathan Shapiro she would be home by two. She had also told him she had a date for lunch. But that had been only a convenient excuse for escape from Annabelle Jones and her talk of "rubbish" and her eagerness to learn what the "rubbish" might sell for. Over the counter, presumably. Probably, Dorian thought, Annabelle had been very pretty once and her prettiness had filled a painter's eyes and ——

She stopped abruptly before a canvas which was larger than most of the others and better lighted than any of them. It was "Cityscape"—a portrait, recognizable but imagined, of a city rushing toward the sky. Buildings were blocks and pointing fingers and from somewhere not defined sunlight touched the tops of the tallest. But the sunlight was not really from any actual sun. Nor were the buildings of any city colored so, except in some one's dreams of a city which transcended cities.

Dorian stood in front of the picture and wished it were hers to live with. It would not be a spot of color anywhere; it would not bring contentment; it would not be ignored. Quite possibly it could not be lived with, would never reduce itself even to the surface conformity which is an essential part of living from day to day. Its colors would not be peaceful with any of the colors in the apartment. It was absurd to think of buying it.

She leaned closer. The slip of pasted paper on which a price had been typed was fresher here, and the typing very black and clear. "$1,500" was the price. Quite absurd to think of buying it. She moved back from it and kept on looking at it, and gradually a faint sense of familiarity built into her mind. It was not familiarity with this painting. She had never seen this painting. The familiarity was recognition of a style—of brushwork, of a way of laying color on.

Taped to the wall beside most of the other paintings was a

typed slip on which the painter was named. There was no such identification of the painter of this upward-rushing city.

She leaned closer to the painting and sought a signature, and for a minute or two sought it without success. Then, finally, a series of brush strokes which had seemed part of the composition–part of the base of one of the soaring buildings–took on a shape of its own. Even then she could not be entirely certain. She herself signed her work clearly; the "Hunt" was entirely legible. But many who work on canvas or on drawing paper prefer rather to intimate than reveal their identity.

The brush strokes concealed in the composition might spell "Shack." She thought they did. And under what might be the signature of Shackleford Jones there was a squiggle which might be a date. If it was, it was the date of the year before. She continued to study the signature, and became almost certain, but not entirely certain, that the painter had signed it "Shack." She was surprised. She had told Nathan Shapiro that she thought Shackleford Jones would not sell to a store's gallery. Unless, of course, he needed the money very badly. She would have to tell Shapiro that she was no longer nearly so certain.

A tall dark-haired man, dressed with elegance–and looking a little like a maitre d' of Dorian's acquaintance–came into the room accompanying, and guiding, a small plump woman in a flowered dress. She wore a hat. She somewhat reminded Dorian of Mrs. Isabelle Jones of Emporia, Kansas.

"Something about three feet wide by four feet tall," the woman said. Her voice was assured, and carried. "There will have to be blue in it."

The two went to the end of the room and stood in front of a painting of an ocean. Fortunately, it was a blue ocean. A sandy beach, which was reasonably sand colored, shelved down to the suitably blue ocean. In the foreground there was a beach umbrella. It was red.

The elegant man took a flat cylinder from his pocket and unwound a metal tape and measured the ocean. "Three-six by three," he said, and looked over the dumpy woman at Dorian and smiled and raised eyebrows. Dorian Weigand shook her head and smiled the smile of a woman who is only looking. He nodded welcome to that, but continued for some seconds to look at Dorian, his eyes slightly narrowed.

"Four feet would fit better," the plump woman said. "But it is a very pretty blue. And the ocean looks so real, doesn't it?" She moved closer to the ocean and looked at its price tag. She said, "It's really more than I planned to spend. And not being really the right size. On the other hand . . ."

Dorian thought there might be a good many "other hands" and that she would not wait to ask the salesman if "Shack" had really painted the soaring city. She was, she decided, sure enough he had, and decided that if she was to get any lunch and be home by two, in case Nathan Shapiro called by two, she had better get about it.

She lunched in the tea room on the third floor of Bryant & Washburn, an experience she had resolutely avoided when she worked as a staff artist in the advertising department and had done, always against a deadline, such sketches of "little prancers" as Sally Painter now supplied.

The windows on the second floor of the house in Gay Street were closed although it was becoming an afternoon which warmly asked for open windows. Apparently Rachel Farmer did not mind the heat, or had gone out and closed windows against the late afternoon thundershowers tentatively predicted. Or perhaps her apartment was air-conditioned.

The windows of the floor above were open and somebody was playing a piano beyond them. Nathan Shapiro looked up at the open windows and listened to the music. A show tune, with lilt in it. One Shapiro had never heard before. He climbed three red-stone and gritty steps to the front door of the house and, in the entry-hall, pressed the button marked BRISKIE.

The music stopped in mid-phrase and the door buzzer rasped. Shapiro climbed two flights of stairs and a door was open for him and a tall woman in a two-piece bathing suit looked at him and said, "Oh," with disappointment in the sound. Then she said, "What do you want this time?"

She was, Shapiro guessed, about five feet ten. She had an oval face—a face now twice familiar to Shapiro. Her hair was deeply brown, as it had been in the painting of her in the studio, and her eyes were brown. There were lines from nostril corners to upper lip and they were, Shapiro thought, the kind of lines which deepen. There had been no lines in the painted face. But it was the same face, and almost a lovely one. Her body, nearly as revealed now as it had been to Shack Jones when he had painted it, curved luxuriantly and her legs were straight and long. Particularly good calves, Shapiro thought.

She said, "Well?"

Shapiro told Dorothy Briskie, professionally Dorothy Goodbody, that one or two things had come up and that he was sorry to have to bother her.

"I don't know that you're going to," she said. Her voice had been low and soft the evening before. Now there was an edge to it. "I'm working. Benny's supposed to be here. I thought you were Benny. With the new lyrics."

Nathan Shapiro remained sorry to have to interrupt her work. He would make the interruption as brief as he could.

"The thing is," he said, "there seem to be discrepancies, Mrs. Briskie. We thought you might want to clear them up."

She did not know what he was talking about.

"Just something that doesn't quite jibe," Shapiro said. "Has to do with a painting Mr. Jones did, Mrs. Briskie. A painting of you, I think. Has a number on it—catalogue number, I'm told. The number's seventy-nine."

"The stinker," Dorothy Briskie said. "The lousy stinker. He promised Max and me ——" She stopped abruptly. "I talk too damn much," she said. "Oh, all right. Come on in, then."

The living room into which he followed her seemed smaller than it had the evening before. The compact Baldwin had been pulled out into the middle of the room. It had been against a wall when Shapiro had been there eighteen hours before—had been there and asked a few questions of a small and handsome man who moved like a featherweight boxer and of his much taller wife; had been assured that they both knew Shackleford

Jones only casually, and had never been in his apartment in Eighth Street.

"I see you do remember the picture," Shapiro said in the room which the moved piano seemed to have made smaller. "A very attractive picture, it seemed to me. And what they call representational. Painted, I think, in the living room of his apartment. The model sitting–partly lying–on a striped sofa. In a room you had never visited, Mrs. Briskie."

"It isn't the way it looks," she said. She had sat on the bench in front of the piano when she led him into the room and put long fingers on the keys. Now she turned on the bench to look at him. "Not at all the way it looks, Lieutenant."

"No? How is it, then?"

"All right. The face–all right, the head is mine. The rest–I don't know who posed for that."

One way of telling liars, Shapiro thought, is that they are often so anxiously believable.

"Just the head," he said. "I see. Somebody else's body. Somebody who had been in the apartment. Posed on the sofa. Did he paint there often, Mrs. Briskie?"

"Sketched sometimes," she said. "And coded the colors. He'd finish in the studio. Of course, he knew the colors in the sofa. He carried colors in his head. A good many of them do. He ––"

She stopped herself but not in time. That was recognized between them, with no need of words.

"I talk too damn much," she said.

"Yes, I guess you do, Mrs. Briskie. You said you hardly knew him. Knew him only casually. Had never ––"

"Max said he thought you were trying to make something out of it," she said. "Something not suicide. He said we'd better stay out of it."

"Last night?"

"Just before you came up. All right, I knew him better than I admitted. We both did, actually. But not well enough to help you. That's true. That's absolutely true." There was a good deal of emphasis on the last phrase–the last unnecessary phrase.

"You'd forgotten about the picture? Or thought we wouldn't find it?"

"He promised us–promised me, I mean–he'd destroy it. He said it was just–just sort of a joke."

"The number on it," Shapiro said. "That would be a catalogue number, wouldn't it? The number given it in an exhibit?"

"It wasn't actually hung. Oh, it was and then Maxie found out somehow and Shack took it down. Before the opening. So nobody ever saw it. And the stinker promised ––"

Shapiro waited briefly, but she did not go on.

"Just the head, you say."

"Yes. Not that it would have meant anything anyway. I suppose that's hard for people like you to understand–to believe. I suppose you think that when a woman poses naked for an artist it inevitably ––" She paused. "Leads to something," she said.

Shapiro thought that might well be possible. He did not say so. He thought that Dorothy Briskie had become verbally discreet in midsentence, and that that probably was not characteristic. He did not mention this.

"Your husband wouldn't have objected?"

"Of course not. Any more than I object to his sketching the Farmer girl."

"But he did object to the picture being exhibited?"

"That's a different thing. Entirely different. It would have been–I mean would have seemed to be–a picture of me without any clothes on. Not just a nude. Dorothy Goodbody ––" She half laughed suddenly. "Living up to her name," she said. "His idea of a joke."

"Not yours evidently. And not Mr. Briskie's?"

"No. Would you want your wife–recognizably your wife–painted that way? Or maybe you haven't got a wife."

"I have," Shapiro said. "And the answer is 'No.' But, as you said, 'people like me.' Only, apparently, people like Mr. Briskie, too."

"Because I would be recognized. People would talk. Wait a minute."

She swiveled on the bench and began to play the Baldwin.

Shapiro discovered he was tapping his right foot, and resisting the inclination to hum with the tune. Of course–"The Moon Fell Down." For months, not long before, nobody had been able to turn on a car radio without hearing it. She ended with a sweep of her right hand across the keyboard.

"Yours?"

"Mine and Benny's. And we've got a show set for fall. There's been publicity. Pictures of me. And Benny too, of course. It wouldn't have been a very funny joke, Lieutenant. Not for me, anyway. Leonard Lyons. Maybe even *Variety*. But not for me. You see —"

She stopped again, and then shrugged her bare shoulders and went on.

"This show we're doing," she said, "Benny and I are doing–it's a very wholesome sort. For the family trade. People can take their little brats to it. Like–oh, like *Mary Poppins*. And Hollywood is dickering and–well, Hollywood gets the fidgets."

"Mr. Jones knew about this?"

"Yes, I guess–all right. Yes, he knew about it. I told you he was a stinker sometimes."

"You started to tell me he promised something. To you and Mr. Briskie."

"To destroy it. Anyway, to paint the face out. Nobody would have recognized–I mean, the body isn't my body. I told you that."

She had, of course. For what it was worth. Shapiro sighed. Somebody better at this sort of thing would know whether to press now or let it ride.

"We think," he said, "that Mr. Jones had planned to have a guest Wednesday evening–the evening of the day he killed himself. Or, of course, was killed. You told me last night that you weren't to have been the guest. But also —"

"That was true," she said. "Oh, we both knew him better than we said. But I wasn't going to his apartment Wednesday."

"For the record," Shapiro said, "what did you do Wednesday evening, Mrs. Briskie?"

"Opened a can of something. Or unfroze something. I don't remember. And went to a movie."

"You and your husband?"

She shook her head.

"Max was in Chicago," she said. "With an architect. They got a flight at the crack of dawn. Max maybe will do a mural for the lobby of a new co-op."

"And got back?"

"Yesterday morning. I suppose you want to know whether he got the job?"

Shapiro didn't, especially. But he said, "Did he?"

"He doesn't know yet. So he flew out again this morning to talk to some more people about it."

"Just for the record," Shapiro asked the name of the architect Maxwell Briskie had flown to Chicago with; was, presumably, now in Chicago with. She said he could believe it or not, but she hadn't the faintest idea.

"And if you ask me, he doesn't have the faintest idea who's going to put the show on. My show. And Benny's, of course."

The doorbell rang, the sound loud in the room.

"That'll be Benny," Dorothy Briskie-Goodbody said, and got up from the piano bench. "And we've got work to do."

Shapiro stood up, too. He watched her press a button near the door and heard the rasping from below.

"Did Mr. Jones offer to sell you this painting?" he asked, and walked toward the door. She hesitated, he thought, and then said, "No, he didn't. Anyway, he'd got into the habit of asking the most ——" She stopped with that. Shapiro had no trouble finishing her sentence. He walked on to the door and put his hand on the knob, and heard steps on the stairs. He turned.

"By the way," he said, "have you a key to Jones's studio? Or has your husband?"

There was no hesitancy this time. Her "No" was immediate and emphatic. As if, Shapiro thought, she had anticipated the question.

He opened the door and a medium-sized, plumpish man hurried through it. He carried a large manila envelope and began to wave it at Dorothy Goodbody as he went through the door. When he was inside, Shapiro went outside and down the stairs.

On the second floor, he knocked at Rachel Farmer's door. He knocked several times, but nothing came of it.

VIII

TYPEWRITERS CLATTERED IN the squad room. Detectives spend a good deal of time at typewriters. Nathan Shapiro went through the squad room to his own office, which was a cubbyhole, and a hot one. There were papers in his In basket. A lieutenant of detectives spends a good deal of time reading what others typed.

The police of Emporia, Kansas, had been cooperative. Isabelle Jones was well known in Emporia. Not officially known to the police; known of. Daughter, that was right, of James Cronin, "Cronin, Food Specialities." Lived, alone, on the outskirts of the town, in a house which had been her parents'. Alone because the drive from store to house had, as he grew older, become more than James Cronin wanted to take on. He lived in a small apartment over the store. Emporia was on a feeder airline to Kansas City. Yes, there was a midafternoon flight. It was a short jump to Kansas City; a little over a hundred miles. It was also, of course, not a long drive by car. Mrs. Jones could, obviously, have left her house at any time she chose and driven to Kansas City and got a nonstop plane to New York and, when she chose, a plane back. And picked up her car and returned to her house. There was no reason anybody should have noticed if she had done this, or been concerned. She had neighbors, but they were not close.

There was this, if it was worth anything. "Cronin, Food Specialities" was not what it had been. Partly because James Cronin was somewhere around eighty, and not what he had been thirty years before, when he took the store over from his father. It had been quite a place then, from what one heard of it. Anything in the food line you could buy in Kansas City, and some said New York, you could buy at Cronin's. Foods imported from Europe even. And the meat department—people said that used to be the best in all eastern Kansas. Which said a lot, the Emporia detective thought.

The detective himself, which was to say, for the most part, the detective's wife—not that he was not called in on the marketing on his days off—shopped at a supermarket. And most people did. Even in places a lot bigger than Emporia, the way he heard it, the privately owned, special grocery stores were on their last legs. The chains underpriced them. One thing he did know. Ten years or so before, Cronin's had had a tea room and a lot of the women who shopped in town had gone to it for lunch. But that had been closed down. Yes, rather recently. Yes, there had been some talk that Cronin might have to close the whole place down. Pity if it came to that. Sort of a landmark, Cronin's had been in the old days. From what the detective's parents told him.

Yes, he did know that Belle Jones was married to an artist and not living with him. Man's first name was—wait a minute. He had just thought of something.

Anthony Cook had waited a minute, toll charges the responsibility of New York, New York, not of Emporia, Kansas.

"Piece in the *Gazette,*" the Kansas lieutenant said, after rather more than a minute. "Picked up from the Kansas City *Star*. Headline is, 'Art is Big Business Now.' All about—wait a minute. 'Special correspondence to the Kansas City *Star*.' Yep. About how people have begun to buy paintings all over the country and pay a lot for them. Seems to me—yep. Want me to read what it says about this Jones guy?"

Cook had guessed he did.

"Says," the policeman in the distant state read: "'One of the artists recently most successful is a native of Kansas City, Shackleford Jones, the son of the late Jason Jones, a partner in the wholesale grocery firm of Jones and Hartnett. His paintings, which are for the most part abstractions, are among the most sought after among the works of living modern painters. It is reported in art circles that one canvas, being moved from Mr. Jones's Greenwich Village studio to the gallery of his dealer, was insured for $100,000 during the period of its transit. His dealer, Myra Dedek, declined to confirm or deny this report, but did tell your reporter that there was active interest, on the part of collectors and museums, in the work of Mr. Jones, who always signs himself Shack.' "

The article on art as Big Business had appeared first in the Sunday edition of the *Star*. It was reprinted in the *Gazette* in midweek "by permission." The *Gazette* added that Mr. Jones's wife, Isabelle, lived in Emporia and was the daughter of James Cronin, prominent local merchant.

You put two and two together, Nathan Shapiro thought, and as often as not came up with five–came up with almost anything. Mrs. Jones could, obviously, have flown to New York any time she wanted to, and nobody the wiser. She could, for example, have flown Tuesday. Perhaps after she had read in the Kansas City *Star* about the prosperity of her husband? With her father, perhaps, in considerable need of capital?

Anthony Cook had found Mrs. Jones at the Hilton, as promised. She was certainly going to stay in New York until she found out where she stood. She wasn't going to be cheated out of anything. Not if she knew it, and she was going to see that she did know it. You can't trust New Yorkers. She had found that out during the two years she had lived in New York after her marriage. No, she hadn't read anything in the *Star* about her husband. Yes, she took the *Star*. It came by mail, but she didn't read it very much. Hadn't for years, since it came out against Mr. Goldwater.

Mrs. Jones had checked into the Hilton late Thursday evening. She had not had a reservation, but it had been found possible to accommodate her. The rate on her room was fifteen dollars a day.

"Jeremiah Osgood generally considered reputable art dealer, according to informant, member of the staff New York *Times*."

Michael Corrigan, detective (2nd Grade) had written that, and gone on:

"Established present gallery at —— East 57th Street four years ago. Frequently acts as expert appraiser of paintings, according to informant. Specializes in modern art, including paintings by living artists. Not known to have exhibited work of Shackleford Jones, according to informant, who will have to check further to be sure. Difficult to set values of paintings by living artist, informant says. Go by fads. Says no idea whether there'll be a fad for Shackleford Jones, only now he's dead there could be. Says, 'Sometimes that happens.' Says Jones probably under contract to Dedek Galleries, but doesn't know for sure."

The telephone rang on Shapiro's desk. He said, "Lieutenant Shapiro."

"Dorian," she said. "Dorian Weigand. Was I right about the nude? Number seventy-nine?"

"Partly, at any rate. How did you recognize it?"

"Seen her photograph. With a story about a musical she's doing. I remember what things look like. And people. What do you mean, 'partly,' Nathan?"

"She says the head is hers. Denies she posed for the, er, rest. What she says is. . . ." He told her what Dorothy Goodbody-Briskie had told him, and Dorian said, "Hm-m-m." Then she said, "Do you believe her?"

"I don't know," Shapiro said, and considered that. "No," he said, "I don't, Mrs. Weigand. She was wearing a bathing suit outfit. Of course, it was very warm in her apartment."

Dorian laughed briefly. She said, "You recognized the–call it construction?"

"I think she could have been the model. In his apartment. Would he have painted her there, do you think?"

She didn't know. What was the light like in the apartment?

"Not very good. Not a north light, anyway. Fairly dark without the lights on. Would he have painted by artificial light?"

Again she didn't know. Some painters sometimes did. Most wanted daylight–the steady, unaccented light which comes from the north. She would have thought Shack Jones one of those; would have expected him to paint, if not necessarily to draw, only in his studio.

"She denies she was ever in the apartment?" she asked him.

"Not specifically, any longer. She admits she–and her husband too, she says–knew him better than they said last night.

Says they didn't want to be involved. Sort of thing that does happen." He sighed. "Makes needless trouble," he added.

She said she knew it did; said, "After all, Nathan, I'm a cop's wife." Then she said, "It wouldn't have had to mean anything. That he painted her naked, if he did, doesn't have to mean any more than that. Specifically, that he also slept with her. Which might, as you're thinking, have annoyed her husband. To most painters, I think, naked women are just objects. As, to a doctor, naked women are just bodies–ailing bodies." She paused. "Usually," she said.

"Doctors," Shapiro said, "have nurses in the examining room with women patients. But it's more what Briskie might have thought, isn't it? Whether he was right or wrong to be–annoyed?"

"Only," she said, "he's a painter himself. Probably uses nude models."

He did, Shapiro told her. At least one. A Miss Rachel Farmer. Who also had modeled for Shackleford Jones.

"And for photographers," Dorian said. "Usually with clothes on. At least when she was a clothes model for Bryant and Washburn. They tried using photographs for a while. Gave it up, of course."

"Why?"

"Too explicit. Women could tell what the clothes looked like. Bad for sales. Fashion artists sketch dreams. Dreams for Size Twenties who think they will look like Eights if they buy from Bryant and Washburn. Dear, frothy little dreams at one hundred ninety-eight fifty. And sometimes I guess they do buy their dreams, the poor bulgy dears."

Even very nice women, Shapiro thought, can be quite merciless. Especially when they do not bulge, as Dorian Weigand noticeably did not bulge.

"Speaking of prices," Dorian said, "Bryant and Washburn want fifteen hundred for a Jones painting they've got in the gallery."

"But you said you thought —"

"And was wrong," Dorian said. "I thought he would think he was above it, but apparently he didn't. Once, anyway. He sold them a painting of a city, and it's very good, Nathan. Very, very good, I think. Go look at it. He called it 'Cityscape.'"

Shapiro felt he had seen enough of paintings, particularly those signed "Shack," to last for the rest of his life. He said, "Well . . ."

"You don't have to," Dorian Weigand told him, in consoling tones. "You might like it, but you don't have to. Nobody has to like anything."

"I got the idea," Shapiro said, "from something you said, Mrs. Weigand, that the stores didn't charge much for paintings. Fifteen hundred–that seems a good deal."

"It is," Dorian said. "What I think is, they marked it up when they learned he was dead. That happens often enough. Supply and demand and the supply stops. Can be very pleasant for the estate, of course. Is Isabelle Jones going to be the estate?"

He didn't know. It seemed that Jones's dealer had a considerable claim on it.

"Dear Myra Dedek," Dorian said. "By coincidence, Nathan, I'm going up to her gallery now. Why I called you instead of waiting for you to call and tell me what Dorothy Goodbody said about her portrait, Myra called me. She's going to give a show of cartoons and caricatures in September. After they reopen. Wants me to be in it. And wants me to come up this afternoon and talk about arrangements. Which probably means, will I hold out against fifty-fifty, as I did before. The answer is, I will."

"Are arrangements usually made this far ahead?"

"Yes. Sometimes, anyway. And Myra's going to the Cape next week for the rest of the summer. Says she does every summer. She wants me to take my things in before she leaves. So she can start getting the catalogue ready."

"Does she close the gallery? Or have somebody to run it?"

Dorian thought she closed it.

"Probably with a caretaker," Dorian said. "A man named Williams. Probably sets up the first fall shows."

"I've met Mr. Williams," Nathan Shapiro said. "He carries a screwdriver."

"Whatever for?"

"Apparently," Shapiro said, "to take pictures off other people's walls."

Dorian said that it was an interesting occupation, and that she had to run.

When he had hung up, Shapiro spun a report form, with suitable carbons, into his typewriter and sat and looked at it. Chronologically, as was stipulated. Visit to the Weigand apartment. Visit with Mrs. Weigand to the studio of the deceased. Arrival of widow of deceased. Who had been in Emporia, Kansas, when her husband killed himself—or was killed. Who expected to inherit his paintings, and thought them of no value, but who might have read a newspaper story which said they were. Who might have driven from an isolated house to Kansas City, and flown to New York on Wednesday and killed her husband. Whose father needed money. Discovery by Mrs. Weigand of a painting of a naked woman, whose face was that of Mrs. Maxwell Briskie, who denied she had posed for the painting. Interview with Mrs. Briskie and ——

Shapiro reached hands toward the keyboard and pulled them back again. It was too bad, he thought, that Chicago was so large a city. Probably there would be dozens of cooperative apartment buildings under construction there. Perhaps several designed by New York architects. But—many ambitious enough to include murals in lobbies? One way to find out—Detective Captain Leonard Finley, Chicago police. Oh, a good many ways, but Len Finley might be the simplest. Good guy, Shapiro had thought Finley a few months before, in connection with the identification and detention in New York of a man wanted in Chicago. And a good cop.

It took a while to get through to Finley, and Nathan Shapiro spent part of it convincing himself that Finley, if he ever came on, would have blankly forgotten that a man named Nathan Shapiro existed.

"Hiya, Nate," Leonard Finley said. "New York's finest out of their depth?"

Shapiro certainly believed himself to be, but it was too long a subject to go into. He told Finley he could use a hand, and explained where.

"Building permits," Finley said. And then, more loudly, "Jim. Give the Department of Buildings a ring, will you? Joe Buckley would be the best man. Ask him . . ."

"Shouldn't take long," Finley told Nathan Shapiro, after Jim had been instructed. "How's that pretty wife of yours?"

It did not take long. A good many apartment buildings were under construction, some of them large ones. But only one firm of New York architects was involved—Colbert & Halpern, with offices on Park Avenue.

Neither Mr. Colbert nor Mr. Halpern was available, the operator at Colbert & Halpern told Nathan Shapiro. Could somebody else help him?

It took a little while, as Shapiro had assumed it would. But finally a voice said, "Halpern," rather crossly, and Shapiro went through it.

Primarily, it was Mike Colbert's baby. Only, Colbert was in Chicago. Yes, Maxwell Briskie was one of several artists who had been approached about a mural in the lobby. His cartoons looked pretty modern. Probably they'd settle on a nice simple prairie scene. No point in scaring away prospective purchasers of apartments. But it was Mike's baby.

And what brought the police into it?

"Routine checkup," Shapiro said. "We understand Mr. Briskie flew out to Chicago Wednesday. With the architect, was the way we got it. Just checking it out."

"In connection with?"

"Just a routine investigation," Shapiro said. That did not, to his own ears, sound particularly adequate.

"No idea what Briskie may have done," Halpern said. "Except he didn't fly out with Mike Colbert. It was set up that way. That's true. Only Mike got a virus and had to call it off. Or, put it off. Until today, as a matter of fact. They were going to catch an early flight, and so far as I know they did. Look at a wall and see the construction people and talk figures. Give Briskie a chance to make his pitch with them. For what good it will do him, probably."

"You think it won't do him much good?"

"Mike's baby, Lieutenant. His idea, the mural is. Way it worked out, it's a hell of a big wall. Needs something. But if Briskie wants too much . . ."

Shapiro assumed a shrug of shoulders.

Colbert had expected to fly back late that afternoon. Probably wouldn't stop by the office, but would go on to the country. After all, the weekend was coming up. Which reminded Irving Halpern that he had a train to catch.

Shapiro thanked Halpern and hung up. He looked up the telephone number of Maxwell Briskie and, to his surprise, found it listed in the directory. Less to his surprise, the Briskie telephone was not answered.

Shapiro typed for upwards of an hour, using language as terse as official phraseology permitted.

"Wife's statement that Briskie spent Wednesday in Chicago not confirmed," he wrote, toward the end. "Did not fly to Chicago with architect as she stated. His whereabouts at the time of Jones's death therefore —"

His telephone rang.

A Mr. Maxwell Briskie was at the precinct desk downstairs and wanted to see Lieutenant Shapiro in reference to the Shackleford Jones case.

Mr. Briskie was, by all means, to be sent up.

IX

On the house telephone, George was doubtful. He would certainly do what he could. But Mrs. Weigand knew how it was at this time in the afternoon.

Dorian did know. In late afternoons, just when they are needed most, the taxicabs of New York tend to light their *Off Duty* signs and run for home garages. They re-emerge later with night-shift drivers, but the hiatus remains inconvenient. When Dorian reached the sidewalk in front of the apartment house, George was in the middle of the street, blowing hard on his whistle. And nothing was coming of it.

He came to her shaking his head. He could call the garage and have Mrs. Weigand's car sent around. Perhaps he had better do that, if Mrs. Weigand was in a hurry.

If there is one thing more difficult in late afternoon than achieving a taxicab it is parking a car. Dorian walked the several crosstown blocks to the reserved small building, faced with what might well be marble, which housed the Dedek Galleries. She opened the reticent green door and went into a large, cool room. There was nobody in the room. A few paintings hung on the neutrally painted walls. It was all pointedly noncommercial. It was true that, when she opened the door, Dorian had heard a bell tinkle discreetly somewhere.

She looked at pictures while she waited, which is always a good thing to do while one waits. Then she remembered something and went to the end of the room where, she was almost certain, two paintings by Shackleford Jones hung, and had hung for rather a long time.

There were no paintings by Shackleford Jones on the wall she looked at. She had, Dorian decided, been wrong about the wall on which the Shack paintings hung, waiting for a purchaser. Probably they were in one of the upstairs exhibit rooms.

Behind her, somebody made a small sound which was a rather artificial clearing of the throat. Dorian turned to face a tall man, immaculately dressed to the point of a waistcoat, and with a carefully tended beard. He asked whether he could help madame. He had what seemed to her an inordinately cultivated voice.

Dorian said, "Mrs. Dedek?"

"I'm not sure she is free at the moment," the tall youngish man said. "If madame has some particular picture in mind, I —"

"I have an appointment with Mrs. Dedek," Dorian said. "She telephoned me. My name is Weigand. Oh, Dorian Hunt, professionally."

"Of course," the tall man said. She tried to remember his name. She had just mentioned it to Shapiro—of course. Weldon Williams. One man with a beard tends to look like another man with a beard, if age and structure are reasonably similar. This one would tell Mrs. Dedek that Mrs. Weigand was there. He went across the room and under a staircase which rose out of it. She could hear his voice, muted as, she supposed, he talked on a telephone—a telephone relegated to obscurity under the stairs.

He emerged. If Mrs. Weigand would not mind going up to the office? One flight up, and to the rear.

"My dear Mrs. Weigand," Myra Dedek said, and stood, very trim, behind a period desk, and in front of what was either a Picasso or something very like it. On the wall to her right as she faced Dorian there was a portrait of a can of beans. There was a can-opener beside it. On the opposite wall there was a canvas covered with straight black lines, which seemed vaguely to converge. It looked rather like a chart for the detection of astigmatism.

"Richard Taylor, I hope," Mrs. Dedek said. "And perhaps Steinberg. And three or four others I already have, in the small salon. You'll be in good company. Six of yours, I'd say. Or perhaps more. In September, when people are coming back to town."

It took only a few minutes; agreement was surprisingly easy. Not fifty-fifty. Sixty-forty, with the sixty Dorian's. And catalogue and advertising paid for by the gallery. No exclusive contract with the Dedek Galleries. The show to go on when the gallery reopened in September.

There was, in fact, nothing which could not have been settled on the telephone. Dorian sat in a comfortable chair across the desk from Myra Dedek and fished in her handbag for a pack of cigarettes. Urged, she took a cigarette, instead, from a box Myra Dedek pushed toward her. A "D" was imprinted on the oval cigarette.

"About now," Myra Dedek said, "I usually treat myself to a small glass of sherry. Won't you join me?"

Dorian joined Myra Dedek in a small glass of sherry. She agreed with Myra Dedek that a glass of sherry was relaxing in late afternoon.

"It's a dreadful thing about poor Shack Jones, isn't it?" Myra Dedek said. "So much to live for."

It was a dreadful thing about poor Shackleford Jones.

"You were his dealer, weren't you?" Dorian said. "I seem to remember two of his canvases. I thought they were hanging downstairs."

"They're being cleaned," Myra said. "They'd been hanging there forever. Perhaps now he's dead collectors will be more—appreciative."

Dorian agreed that that was possible, even probable.

"Bryant and Washburn have jumped the price on that one of his they have," Dorian said. "At least, I think they have. The one he called 'Cityscape.' It's a very fine —"

"Bryant and Washburn!" Myra said, and her tone was astonished. "Whatever do you mean?"

"A city rushing up toward the sky," Dorian said. "Give me a sheet of paper."

"I'm sure you're wrong," Myra Dedek said, but slid across the desk a sheet of paper with "Dedek Galleries" printed at the top of it. No, engraved at the top of it.

With quick pencil strokes Dorian sketched on the letterhead planes which reached irregularly toward the sky. (Or, at any rate, toward the words "Dedek Galleries.") She turned the sheet toward Myra Dedek. "The shape of it," she said. "What I remember of the shape of it. At the top a special kind of light."

Myra Dedek looked at the sketch and held it close to her eyes and then farther from them. Then she shook her head.

"Nothing of his I ever saw," she said. "And he wouldn't have sold to a store. Not ever. You must be wrong, Mrs. Weigand. And, he was under contract to me. Was this painting–" she waggled the sheet of paper–"was it signed?"

"A squiggle. But I'm quite sure it spelled 'Shack.' "

Myra Dedek shook her head again, and again studied the sketch Dorian had made.

"You can't tell anything from that," Dorian said. "I realize that."

"The composition," Myra said. "Not at all like his, really. More like ––" She leaned back in her chair and looked at the ceiling. "It does remind me of someone," she said. "I can't at the moment–wait, I think I can. A new man named Shayburn. Did a good many city scenes. And 'Shayburn' could look like 'Shack,' couldn't it? The way they scrawl?"

"The brushwork," Dorian said. "The–oh, the feel of it."

"They derive from each other," Myra said. "Especially when they're starting in or just groping around for a style. Shayburn was quite young. You're familiar with Jones's work?"

"I've seen a good deal of it," Dorian said, and did not amplify.

"He varied more than most," Myra Dedek said. "And lately–was there a date on this painting you thought was his?"

"Yes. Last year."

Myra looked again at the rough sketch Dorian had made to indicate the composition of the "Cityscape"; the upward thrust of it.

"It has movement," she said. "A great deal, really. From your version." She continued to look at the sketch, and also to talk. "He was static last year," she said. "Shack, I mean. It was part–part of his going downhill, really. Being painted out. Which was, I'm afraid, the reason he did such a dreadful thing. Killed himself."

She put the sketch face down on her desk and lighted a cigarette.

"I told some detective that," she said, and now looked across the desk at Dorian. "Your husband is a police officer, isn't he?"

Dorian nodded her head.

"It seems so strange," Mrs. Dedek said, "that they don't accept the obvious. I suppose it's merely that they're not allowed to. Isn't that it?"

"They have to make sure."

"You know," Myra said, "I found his body. It was–dreadful. I'd gone to look at his new work. Things he'd done while he was in Spain. And he was on the floor with blood all around and–and a revolver on the floor just beyond his hand. Where it had fallen after he shot himself." She covered her eyes with a hand, the movement abrupt. "I'll never get it out of my mind," she said. "Never. *Never!*"

She seemed to shiver momentarily.

"I know it's a dreadful thing," Dorian said. "It will fade out."

"It was so obvious what had happened," Myra Dedek said. "I can't understand why . . ."

She left the sentence unfinished and straightened her trim body in the chair.

"I'm sorry," she said. "It's nothing to bother you with, is it? About this picture at the store. That's something it's easy enough to straighten out." She looked at the watch on her wrist. She said, "Oscar'll still be there," and reached to her telephone and spun the dial. The number she wanted apparently was ready in her mind.

She said, "Good afternoon. Extension four twenty-one, please." There was a moment of waiting. Dorian could hear the telephone crackling to itself. Then Myra said, "Mr. Bracken, please" and, after a moment, "I'll hold on."

"Oscar Bracken," she said, and put a hand over the mouthpiece. "He's the curator there. Or whatever they call it at the stores. *Yes, I'm waiting.* It's quite all right. Used to be here with me, you know. *Yes, I'm holding on.* Much more knowledgeable than poor Weldon will ever be. Not that Weldon doesn't do all he can. Isn't the most loyal soul–*Oscar. Myra Dedek. Oh, fine. The thing is . . .*"

The thing was that a friend of hers had seen a painting in the Bryant & Washburn gallery that she thought was one of Shackleford Jones's. She knew it couldn't be, but . . .

There was the sound of a man's voice from the telephone. The words were indistinguishable.

"Yes," Myra said. "It's really dreadful. About this painting—it's called 'Cityscape,' my friend says. And she thought she recognized the signature as Shack's. I told her that wasn't possible. That Shack never sold to the stores. It's—oh, say to settle a bet. He never did, did he?"

This time Dorian could distinguish the words of the answer. "Not to us," the man said.

"You know the picture she means?"

The deeper voice sounded again. The words were no longer distinguishable.

"From the description she gives me, that's the one," Myra said. She began to nod her head, still holding the phone to her ear. "I was sure that was it," she said. "I win my bet, don't I? I thought it might be a Shayburn. I knew it couldn't be Shack."

The male voice rumbled again.

"I know you know about the contract, Oscar," Myra said. "I know Bryant and Washburn wouldn't dream. And that you of all people wouldn't, Oscar. I know how careful you are. Who better?"

The male voice again; the words indistinguishable again.

"Perhaps the styles are a little similar," she said. "I'll tell my friend that. Has anybody else made the same mistake?"

Dorian could hear the answer this time. The answer was, "No."

"Not anybody?"

"Not anybody."

Myra Dedek hoped she had not dragged Oscar Bracken away from a customer. She knew how hard customers were to come by in the summer. She said, "And *you* take care, Oscar," and put the telephone in its cradle.

"Shayburn," she said needlessly. "Dear Oscar says the styles are similar and that the signatures might be anything. Even to an eye as good as yours, dear. It's a perfectly natural —"

The telephone rang and Myra picked it up. Again the sound from the receiver was the scratch of a male voice.

"Yes, Weldon," Myra Dedek said. "I think we may as well. Of course, we mustn't lock Mrs. Weigand in, must we? And you'll remember about the alarm, won't you? And to switch the phone to my apartment?"

She said, "Good night, then," and put the telephone back in its cradle and stood up behind her desk. Dorian crushed her cigarette out in a tray and stood too. Myra Dedek was glad, so very glad, that some of Mrs. Weigand's work would be in the exhibit. Mrs. Weigand–"I always think of you as Dorian Hunt, really"–must choose for the show only the things she herself liked best.

And–would it be at all possible for her to send them around the next day? Ten or twelve to choose from, if she had so many she wanted to show. So that, during the rest of the summer, she–"and dear Weldon, of course"–could get to work on the catalogue and the advertising? So that everything would be ready when the gallery reopened in September? She realized the notice was short, but . . .

Dorian could.

There was no one in the downstairs showroom. Weldon Williams was, presumably, setting the burglar alarm. Dorian went out of the sedate four-story building which housed the Dedek Galleries.

Weldon Williams was not setting the alarm. He was standing by the curb, evidently looking for a taxi with its roof light on. Two came in sight and he waved and the first one pulled in, stopping the other behind it and itself stopped by traffic ahead. Williams said, "Here you are, Mrs. Weigand. Just in time," and opened for her the door of the first cab. For a moment, Dorian thought he was about to take her arm, assist her into the low cab. He stopped short of that, but he closed the door for her and smiled and nodded at her through the open window.

The taxi still was blocked. Dorian looked at her watch. It was a little before five; Bryant & Washburn would be open for half an hour. She said, "Bryant and Washburn, please," to the taxi driver, who turned in his seat and said, "Where, lady?" She repeated her directions.

"You've got Dotty all upset," Maxwell Briskie told Shapiro as he entered Shapiro's cubbyhole. Then he turned with quick grace and said, "Thanks, officer," to the uniformed patrolman who had shown him the way to the headquarters of Homicide, South. He took three steps needed to bring him to Shapiro's desk and stood in front of it and smiled down at the long-faced man. Shapiro said, "Sit down, Mr. Briskie. Sorry I disturbed your wife. How?"

"All this fuss about the painting poor old Shack did of her. Feels she gave you the wrong impression about that. Left you feeling we were annoyed with Shack about it." He sat in the wooden chair Shapiro indicated. "And that you're looking around to find people who were annoyed with Shack. *Ergo,* that you don't think he killed himself." He continued to smile cheerfully across the desk. "Be simpler that way, wouldn't it?"

"Yes," Shapiro said. "I did get the impression you were both, as you put it, annoyed with Mr. Jones about the painting of your wife. Just of your wife's face, she says."

"Attack of modesty," Briskie said. "Of course she posed for the figure, too. Why not?"

Shapiro sighed.

"I don't know, Mr. Briskie," he said. "Why did she deny it?"

"Thought you'd get wrong ideas," Briskie said. "Think there was something–let's call it personal–involved. You do think somebody killed Shack?"

"We're looking into the possibility," Shapiro said.

"Of course you are," Briskie said. "Sticks out a mile, wouldn't you say? *Ergo,* looking for suspects. Suspects with motives. She posed for the picture. Thinks you might take that to mean she slept with Shack. And that I got annoyed and plugged him. Do you think that, by the way?"

"We're investigating a good many possibilities," Shapiro told him. "Not jumping to any conclusions. I take it you didn't come here to confess, Mr. Briskie?"

Briskie laughed at that.

"To murder? Not likely, is it? For the record—I wasn't jealous of Shack. For the same record, wouldn't have shot him if I had been. Might have cuffed him around a bit. I suppose you think I couldn't have?"

"I've no idea," Shapiro said. He thought the quick small man who sat opposite him was disappointed by that. Small men are often sensitive. Shapiro softened it. "I take it you've been a boxer, Mr. Briskie?"

"Few years ago," Briskie said. "Amateur. Featherweight. It isn't always a matter of size, Lieutenant."

"No," Shapiro said. "That's what you came to tell me, Mr. Briskie? That you weren't jealous of Mr. Jones? Didn't kill him. Because you thought your wife's not very convincing denial that she had posed in the nude for Mr. Jones would give a conventional person like me the wrong idea?"

"Mincing word, 'nude,'" Briskie said and looked thoughtfully at Shapiro. "Or did I say that before? As to the other, I thought things could do with a bit of straightening out."

It could hardly, to Nathan Shapiro, have been put more mildly. He said, "Thanks for coming in, Mr. Briskie. Good idea to straighten things out. Anything else you want to straighten out?"

Briskie looked at him intently, his eyes narrowed.

"You think there's something else?" he said, after he had, seemingly, studied Shapiro's long, sad face. His voice, which had been noticeably cheerful, changed; became deeper.

"I gather you do," Briskie said.

"Yes," Shapiro said. "Wednesday, Mr. Briskie. The day you weren't in Chicago. Another false impression your wife might have given me, wasn't it?"

"What did you do?" Briskie asked. "Check flight passenger lists?"

"Talked to a Mr. Halpern," Shapiro said. "About you and Mr. Colbert. Who came down with a virus. Do you want to consult counsel, Mr. Briskie? You have the right, you know. The Supreme Court's rather firm about it."

Again Briskie looked at him intently across the desk. Then he shook his head.

"Believe it or not," he said, "I've no reason to hide behind anything–lawyer or law or anything. Also, Shack was a damned good painter, for my money. If somebody killed him ––" He ended that with a shrug of his shoulders.

"All right," Shapiro said. "Where were you Wednesday?"

"Several places," Briskie said. "Kennedy International, where Colbert caught up with me by phone and called it off. In my studio, working. I've got a loft a couple of blocks from where Shack had his. And–O.K., in Shack's studio. And he was fine when I talked to him and when I left him. No holes in him."

"Again," Shapiro said, "so you'll be straight about it. You don't have to tell me anything."

"That easy?"

"Well," Shapiro said, "if I got the idea you were withholding material information I could ––"

"I know," Briskie said. "The material witness bit. All right. I decided to drop by and make another pitch. About this painting of Dotty. Because he'd planned to show it once and ––" He shrugged again. "You couldn't tell what Shack might decide to do next," he said. "If he decided it was good for Shackleford Jones. So . . ."

So, he told Shapiro, he had decided to have one more go at buying the painting and had gone to Jones's studio on the chance he might be there. There was no good–there was never any good –in trying to get Shack on the telephone. Unless he expected a call, he didn't answer the telephone.

There was no sign *Go Away* on Jones's door and the door was not locked. Under those circumstances, one pulled the door open and went in. Briskie pulled the door open and went in, and Jones was standing in front of an easel working on a sketch.

"One of Miss Farmer?"

It could have been. Most of the time Shack wasn't representational. "The one of Dotty was an exception." Anyway . . .

Shackleford Jones had turned from his work and said, "Now who the–oh, it's you, Maxie. I'm not taking any pupils today."

Which had been, Briskie explained, a gag. It was, with Jones, rather a running gag for fellow painters. He thought it was funny, and his friends pretended to. Not, usually, with any special enthusiasm.

"All right," Briskie said–now told Shapiro he had said–"what's the least you'll take for it, Shack?"

Shack had, for a moment only, pretended he did not know what Briskie was talking about. But then he said, "Oh, still fussing about that picture of Dotty?"

Briskie said, "How much, Shack?"

It was good, Shackleford Jones told him; damned good. Look good on any wall.

"Wall behind a bar," Briskie told him. "How much, Shack?"

"Ought to ask you five thousand," Shack Jones said. "Especially after that crack. You're the one who paints murals, Maxie. Anyway, you probably haven't got five thousand. What about five hundred?"

It was, Maxwell Briskie told Shapiro, more than he and Dotty wanted to pay. He had told Jones that. But it was not more than they could pay to avoid the "snickering" which would go about town if Jones showed the picture. They had, however, finally settled on three hundred, with the stipulation that the signature be painted out. "Because you might leak it out that you'd got a Shack for a measly three hundred."

The picture wasn't, obviously, one to carry unwrapped through the streets. Jones thought he had wrapping paper somewhere, and started toward the rear of the studio to find it. He was halfway down the long loft when the telephone rang. He went on, more quickly, and out of Briskie's sight, behind a canvas on one of the easels. But he was not out of hearing.

Shackleford Jones said, "Oh, it's you, is it?" To Briskie he had sounded annoyed. There was an interval during which Briskie assumed the caller was talking. Then Jones said, "Come along then. And see that you can," and put the receiver back and, Briskie thought, put it down hard. Then Jones came back up the studio. "He always," Briskie said, "walked as if he owned the earth."

"Can't fool around wrapping it up now," Jones said, when he was halfway up the studio. "Got somebody coming. Come back tomorrow and get the damn picture. And bring a check."

"He was peremptory as hell," Maxwell Briskie told Shapiro. "As if, all of a sudden, he was sore about something. I said, 'How about this afternoon?' and he said, 'Tomorrow, like I said. If you really want it.' I didn't want to rub him the wrong way, at least until I got the picture."

So Briskie said–now said he had said–"Tomorrow it is," and left.

"When was this?" Shapiro asked him. "Wednesday morning about when?"

Somewhere around ten, Briskie told him. Probably a little after ten.

"You said he didn't always answer the telephone," Shapiro said. "Unless he expected a call. You think he expected this one?"

"Acted like it."

"And that, after he got the call, he was, as you put it, 'sore about something.'"

"Sounded like it."

"You say 'all of a sudden.' He hadn't been annoyed before?"

"He was always a scratchy sort of bastard. Particularly if he was interrupted while he was working. But no, I'd say he was about at his usual pitch."

"You didn't get the impression he was depressed?"

Briskie had not. After the call he was annoyed, but only that, so far as Maxwell Briskie could tell.

"If you mean, Did he seem like a man who was going to kill himself? the answer is No. Not that I know how a man would act just before he killed himself."

"You didn't go back later that day?"

Briskie had not. He had gone out of the loft building and walked toward his own studio. And . . .

"I suppose I'd better tell you this. So as not to withhold material information. About a block–block and a half–from Shack's place I ran into Rachel Farmer. I said 'Hi' and she said 'Hi, Maxie.' "

"She was going toward Mr. Jones's studio?"

"In that direction. But three or four painters have studios around there. Rent's cheap. God knows it ought to be. She poses for a lot of people. Could have been going anywhere. All right, I did think that perhaps she was the one who had called Shack. And I suppose you think I'm a heel to drag her into it."

Shapiro said he didn't. He did not mention the possibility of red herrings. He said, "I take it you didn't go back the next day? To pay for the picture and pick it up? Why? Because you'd heard, somewhere, that Mrs. Dedek had found Mr. Jones dead?"

"I could say that, couldn't I?" Briskie said. He spoke slowly, and there was uncertainty in his tone, or Shapiro thought there was. "That I heard it on the radio. It was on the radio, you know. Maybe I'd better say that, Lieutenant."

"I wouldn't," Shapiro said, "unless it's true, Mr. Briskie. I take it it isn't true?"

"All right," Briskie said. "I was there, Lieutenant. I–I'm not making myself sound too good, am I? All right. I found him before Myra did. I . . ."

He had gone to Shack's studio a little before ten o'clock Thursday morning. "With a check in my pocket, and a roll of wrapping paper under my arm." Again, the door to the studio was not locked, and again, after knocking and not being answered, Briskie had pulled it open. He had taken two or three steps inside and seen Shackleford Jones's body on the floor. With blood around it. "A hell of a thing to walk in on."

He had, he said, been certain that Shack Jones was dead. "From the way he was lying. You can tell if–well, if somebody's been dead long enough." But, staying as much as he could out of the congealed blood, he had walked to the body to make sure. He had touched one of the dead hands and found it cold. And then, to the surprise of the man he talked to, Briskie seemed momentarily to break up. A kind of shudder went through his slim body; he made both hands into fists and held them before his face.

"Damn it all," he said, and his voice, too, shook. "The hand I touched was the hand Shack painted with. Damn it to hell. The hand he *painted* with."

After a moment he took his own hands down and took a deep breath and then his body no longer shook. "Sorry," he said. "He was a good painter, Lieutenant. Ought to have had years to paint in."

"And to live in," Shapiro said. "Go on, Mr. Briskie."

Certain Jones was dead, Briskie had started toward the rear of the studio and toward the telephone. But then he had turned back and gone to the door and pressed the button which activated the snap lock.

"Damned if I know why I did that," Briskie said and looked at Shapiro, who said, "Don't you, Mr. Briskie?"

There was a considerable pause.

"All right," Briskie said. "I didn't want to be walked in on. Because I thought, I call the police and they start rummaging around and they'll find the picture of Dotty and somebody will recognize it and—well, get the notion Dotty thought you'd got. So . . ."

So he decided to find the picture and wrap it up and get it out of there. After that, he told Shapiro, he was going to telephone the police from some other place. Shapiro could believe that or not.

Nathan Shapiro didn't, particularly. He thought that the Briskies were people who preferred to stay out of unpleasant things, whether they had special reason to or not. He also thought that they were by no means unique in this.

"It didn't work out that way, evidently," Shapiro said. "Because the police were called after Mrs. Dedek found the body. And not by you."

"No," Briskie said, "it didn't work out that way. The way it was . . ."

He had been in the rear of the studio, looking for the picture —"There's a hell of a lot of them, racked all over the place"—and had just found it when he heard a key in the lock of the front door.

He was out of sight, behind a rack of paintings. He stayed out of sight and listened, and heard the door open. Then he had heard somebody—a woman but he had not recognized the voice —call out something like, "Are you here, Shack?" and then the click of a woman's heels on the wooden floor. It had sounded to him as if she walked over to Jones's body.

"Then after maybe a minute she began to scream bloody murder," Briskie said.

He had looked around the rack and seen Myra Dedek. She was standing a few feet from the door, and looking across the room at the body and screaming. Then she had turned and gone back through the doorway to the corridor outside and she had kept on screaming.

And Maxwell Briskie had decided it was a good time to get out of there. The screaming would bring somebody and somebody would call the police.

"And I," Briskie said, "would have a good deal of explaining to do. People who find bodies do, from all I've heard."

He was doing a good deal of explaining now, Shapiro thought. Of course, he had had time to work out an explanation. It might well be that. Now that, because Dorian Weigand had recognized the face of a painted woman from a newspaper photograph, the Briskies had been brought into it.

"So," Briskie said, "I went down the fire escape."

"You didn't try to take the painting with you? The one it was so important for you and Mrs. Briskie to have?"

"No. All right, I thought of trying it. But the picture's too damned big, Lieutenant. And—all right, I'm not. I'll say it before you do."

Shapiro had not planned to say it.

He said, "By the way, Mr. Briskie. Jones wore a beard until lately, didn't he?"

"Very thick," Briskie said. "Very curly. Reddish. A beard you couldn't miss. Very special beard."

"Happen to know when he shaved it off? And why?"

"When he got back from Spain, I guess. Two or three weeks ago. I've no idea why. He'd worn it ever since I knew him. Before a lot of young squirts went in for beards. Maybe he decided it didn't make him stand out any more. He liked to stand out, Shack did."

Briskie sat, evidently waiting for more questions.

"All right, Mr. Briskie," Shapiro said. "A good idea of yours to come in."

"I can go along? No material witness bit?"

"If you don't go too far," Nathan Shapiro told the lithe, quick little man, and watched Maxwell Briskie go.

X

MYRA DEDEK HAD been certain that the painting in the Bryant & Washburn gallery was not by Shackleford Jones. She had been certain of this before she telephoned Oscar Bracken. But she had not seen the picture. She had seen only a hurried sketch meant to suggest the composition. She had, and that was really all it came to, taken the word of a man named Oscar ––

For a moment, Dorian, sitting in a taxicab that edged down Fifth Avenue, dodging buses which unpredictably turned from curbs into traffic, could not at first remember the last name of the man named Oscar, who had confirmed what Myra Dedek was already so sure of. Then it came back to her–Bracken. When she did remember it, it seemed to her that she remembered from a longer time before, not merely from Myra's mention of it minutes ago in her office. A name she ought to know? From . . .

Of course. From the time she had been in a show at the Dedek Galleries. A man named Bracken had been around, as part of the gallery staff. Probably she had met him, been introduced to him. She could not, however, remember what he looked like. The tall man who had measured a seascape for a potential customer? The one she had thought looked vaguely like a maitre d' in a restaurant to which she and Bill sometimes went? It was all most fuzzy.

"This will do," Dorian told the cabdriver when they were a block from the Bryant & Washburn building, and seemed likely to remain there indefinitely. She had to repeat what she said more loudly; the cabdriver was evidently deaf. She paid and got out of the cab, and walked the block.

As she went into the store, she was mildly irked with herself. There was no reason to think that Myra Dedek had been wrong about the painting and she herself right. (But Myra had not seen it.) There was no reason to think that Bracken had lied about it. If he had a Shack Jones up for sale he would certainly not deny it. I'm not an expert, Dorian told herself. Merely, in this field, a buff. After looking at so many of Shack's paintings I've probably begun to see them everywhere.

At this hour, I'll never get a taxi home. Bill may, for once, get home early–get home to an empty apartment.

What it comes to, Dorian thought, is that I'm merely being stubborn about a hunch. Oscar Bracken is an experienced and honest man; Myra Dedek is an expert and knowledgeable dealer. I'm only a buff with a tattered hunch. I'll look at a cityscape again and satisfy myself. And then start a fruitless search for a taxicab.

But when she went into Bryant & Washburn's she walked its extensive first floor–where a few customers hesitated and tired saleswomen were as patient as a long day had left them–to the executive elevators. One of them was still running. It took her to the eighth floor.

Ursula Fields's secretary had lowered her typewriter into her desk and was putting her gloves on, having just replenished her lipstick. Mrs. Fields had gone for the day. She had gone for the weekend. If Mrs. Weigand would like to make an appointment for Monday?

Mrs. Weigand would not. She went down a corridor to the smaller office of Nancy Sperling, art director. Nancy's receptionist had gone. Nancy herself had not. She was standing in the doorway of her office and talking to a much taller and very thin young woman and shaking her head as she talked. To Dorian she said, "Hello, dear. You remember Rachel Farmer from the old days? When she used to pose for Billy?"

Billy–Billy Weston–had done photographs for Bryant & Washburn before the advertising department abandoned the representational as too much so.

Dorian said, "Of course," which was the easier of two answers. (The other would have been, "Not at all.") "Good afternoon, Miss Farmer."

Rachel Farmer said, "Hello," as if she did not mean it. She

said to Nancy Sperling, "Then I've wasted my time?" and Nancy said, "I'm afraid so, dear. I don't know how the rumor got started."

Rachel Farmer said, "Damn," and strode past Dorian and out of the office.

"She heard somewhere we were looking for photographer's models," Nancy said. "Wanted to get in on the ground floor. Don't tell me you've done the buyer and the pants already."

"Haven't touched them," Dorian said. "The man who heads up the art gallery here. Man named Oscar Bracken. Do you know him?"

"To speak to. Why? Don't tell me you're going to sell pictures to Bryant and Washburn?"

Dorian was not. She had had a look through the gallery and wondered about the man who ran it. It sounded thin to her own ears and, from Nancy Sperling's smile and slightly lifted shoulders, she thought it sounded so to Nancy. But Nancy was tolerant of those who worked with pencils and with brushes. In her job she needed to be.

"Specifically?" Nancy said.

"Is he good? I mean, does he know about paintings? Or is there a buying department which decided what goes into the gallery?"

As far as Nancy Sperling knew, the gallery was Oscar Bracken's. As long as it showed a profit, of course. As to his being good at it—"All employees of Bryant and Washburn are certified, dear. By Personnel."

Dorian said, "Give, Nancy."

Nancy Sperling had, she said, nothing to give. Not really. Oscar Bracken was tall and dark-haired and, at a guess, somewhere in his forties. He had, she thought, been head—he was called "curator"—of the art gallery since Bryant & Washburn had decided to give art a fling. Which was about two years ago. She had heard somewhere that, before he was hired by the store, he had worked in a gallery. Fifty-seventh Street place. Or Madison Avenue. Presumably, Personnel had been convinced that he knew his job. "Which is, primarily, to buy pictures for about half what he thinks they can be sold for. To people who think living-room walls look bare without pictures on them."

"Presumably," Dorian said, "he knows about pictures. Enough, anyway. And about painters? Which ones have caught on with the critics? And with the museums? Which ones haven't?"

"I don't suppose," Nancy Sperling said, "that Bryant and Washburn competes much with the Museum of Modern Art. Or the Metropolitan. What is all this, Dorian? No–wait. Don't tell me. A painter named Shackleford something is shot in his studio, apparently a suicide. A woman named Dorian Weigand is the wife of a policeman. What are you, dear? A member of the Ladies' Auxiliary of the New York Police Department?"

"I'm curious about something," Dorian said. "That's all it is, really."

Nancy Sperling said, "Hm-m-m." Then she said, "You know what they used to say about you when you were here? With the best of envy. That you moved like a cat. Don't let your curiosity carry you too far, darling. Anyway, until you've done the buyer and the pants."

"Promised," Dorian said.

"I'm sorry I can't be more help about Mr. Bracken. Personnel could, if it wanted to. But Personnel will be gone for the day. For the weekend, probably. If you like ——" She gestured toward the telephone on her receptionist's desk, a desk obviously closed for the weekend, like Personnel. And as she gestured, she looked at the watch on her wrist.

"Oh," Dorian said, "I'm going, dear."

She went. She went down on the escalator to the furniture department and through it, in a course now familiar, to the art gallery. It still was open. There were even several people in it. And one of them was the rather dumpy little woman from Emporia, Kansas.

Mrs. Isabelle Jones was looking at pictures–moving along one of the walls and looking at each of the canvases hung on it. She leaned close to the pictures and looked at them carefully. After she had looked, she wrote briefly in a notebook.

Dorian watched her for a moment, puzzled. Titles of pictures. Why? She seemed . . .

Mrs. Jones held her hands apart at the width of a picture and then at the distance of its depth. She looked at the space between her hands with both—of course, with both measurements. She made notes in her little book. She leaned closer to a picture and Dorian realized she was not looking at the picture as picture. She was looking at the price tag.

Prices and measurements. How much art was going at per square foot. Mrs. Jones was comparison shopping. If a picture measuring two feet by four is offered at two hundred and seventy-five dollars, the—approximately acres of, Dorian thought—canvases in the studio in Little Great Smith Street could be measured. Eight square feet—two hundred and seventy-five dollars. Eighty, therefore, two thousand seven hundred and fifty. Mrs. Jones was, potentially, taking inventory.

Mrs. Jones measured and noted the price of another picture. She was very intent.

Dorian went along the other wall to look, once more and more carefully, at a painting of a soaring city; to look, very carefully indeed, at the signature which she had—assuming the honesty and competence of a man named Oscar Bracken—mistakenly thought that of Shackleford Jones, deceased.

The picture called "Cityscape" was not on the wall. Where Dorian was certain it had been, there was a larger canvas; a portrait of, presumably, an ancestor. Female. The subject had worn an evening dress and rested the fingers of her left hand delicately on a table. The table looked very like a table. The fingers did not look too much like fingers. Hands are, for a good many, hard to draw.

For an instant, Dorian's own fingers itched for a familiar pencil. Or for a brush. A quick line here and another there. Professionals are easily tempted toward revision, whether it is their concern or not.

So the painting, which wasn't a Shack, but by someone named Shayburn, was no longer available to be looked at carefully, so that an unsupported hunch would quit rustling in a mind.

A tall man with his back to her was standing in front of the painting titled "Foster, Missouri" and for a moment she thought that the man was Oscar Bracken. But he turned his head a little and, seeing his profile, she realized he was not Bracken. Bracken had probably gone for the weekend, too.

She looked around the room and saw a door with a plaque on it–*Oscar Bracken, Curator*. The door was closed. There would be no harm in knocking on it. There would be no harm in asking the whereabouts of a picture called "Cityscape," and sounding, as much as possible, like a possible customer.

She crossed to the door and was about to knock when she heard voices from behind it. Mr. Bracken was still there, presumably. He was not alone, but talking to someone. He was answered, the words indecipherable. Another man. A real customer, probably. A painter with a picture to sell, possibly. A conference to break in on?

She hesitated, and as she did so there was movement beyond the door and then the door was pushed open. As it opened, but only partly, it opened toward Dorian, so that she was behind it. Oscar Bracken poked his head out and said, pitching his voice across the room, "Be with you in just a moment, Mr. Osgood."

The tall man who had been appraising the picture titled "Foster, Missouri," waved a casual hand in response.

Bracken drew back into his office and closed the door.

Osgood? Jeremiah Osgood, art dealer? Contemplating a purchase from the art gallery of Bryant & Washburn? At first it seemed unlikely. After a moment it seemed quite possible. The store galleries did, sometimes, buy the early work of painters who might, later, turn out to be successful–men and women worthy of the attention of the owners of galleries like Jeremiah Osgood, Inc. Or, for that matter, Myra Dedek, not "Inc." Mr. Osgood might be scouting.

The door of Oscar Bracken, Curator, opened again, this time more widely. Again Dorian was behind it when it was open.

The man who came out of it was not Bracken, but Weldon Williams. He did not stop to look at pictures, or at anybody else in the room–not at Isabelle Jones, still noting down prices and estimating measurements; not at Osgood. He walked across the room like a man in a hurry, and out of it.

He had left the office door open behind him and Bracken came out and walked across the room to stand by Osgood. Osgood pointed at "Foster, Missouri." He said, "The young man can paint, Oscar. Happen to have any more of his around?"

"We discover them; Jeremiah Osgood, Inc., steals them," Bracken said. But he was cheerful about it. "Yes, we have one or two others. Yes, he can paint. I suppose now you want his address? And telephone number?"

"Certainly," Jeremiah Osgood said. "If he has more, and they're as good as this, I might talk to him about a show."

Bracken shrugged his shoulders.

"We won't stand in his way," he said. "I'll go . . ."

He turned with that and then, for the first time apparently, saw Dorian Weigand.

"I'll see you get his address," he told Osgood. "Get it in the mail Monday."

"Appreciate it," Osgood said and looked again at "Foster, Missouri" and nodded his head. Then he went toward the doorway leading out of the gallery.

And Mrs. Isabelle Jones put her notebook in her handbag and went after him. She went, Dorian thought, as if she planned to catch up with him.

"Can I help you?" Oscar Bracken said to Dorian, in the tone of an attentive salesman to a possible customer. But he looked at the watch on his wrist. "Or would you like to look around?"

"I was in earlier," Dorian said. "There was one painting over there." She gestured the direction. "Quite large. What is called modern, I think. A painting called 'Cityscape.' My husband and I are just furnishing a new apartment and there's a wall space it would fit on. At first I thought the price was too high but I talked to my husband and ––"

She stopped because Oscar Bracken was sadly shaking his head.

"I'm sorry," he said. "Really very sorry, madame. The picture you're talking about has been sold, I'm afraid. If it's a matter of dimensions, we have a number of excellent pictures . . ."

This time it was Dorian who shook her head.

"The colors would have been so right in the room," she said, and put–hoped she put–disappointment in her voice. "And it was–I don't know how to put it. Exciting? Of course, I don't know anything about art, really."

He said, "Appreciation of art is subjective, Mrs. ––" He stopped there, but Dorian was almost sure that a name was in his mind, and that it was the correct name. So the charade she was acting out was a little absurd. But she had started it. "I'm very sorry," Bracken added. "Actually, it had already been sold when you saw it earlier, I'm afraid. We just hadn't gotten around to taking it down."

Dorian said "tchk," or thereabouts, remaining the housewife with a blank wall in a new apartment.

"Have you anything similar by the same artist?" she asked Bracken. "Something about the same size? I'm afraid I didn't notice the artist's name."

"Shayburn," Bracken said. "Alan Shayburn. No, I'm afraid we haven't, Mrs. . . . madame."

"If he has a studio in New York," Dorian said, "perhaps I could see him and–or isn't that the way it's done, Mr. ––?" She made something of a point in looking at the door with a name on it. She said, "Bracken."

"He hasn't. Here or anywhere, I'm sorry to say," Bracken said. "The painting you liked was done two or three years ago. He moved to Arizona. For his health. He died there about a year ago."

"How sad," Dorian said. "He painted well, didn't he? I'd–I guess I'd set my heart on that picture. And my husband said I should go ahead and buy it. He's very generous about things like that. But fifteen hundred dollars seemed rather a lot. Most of the pictures you have are a good deal less expensive, aren't they? Was Mr. Shayburn a famous artist? Like the one I read about in the paper this morning? Because he'd killed himself."

"Shackleford Jones," Bracken said. "Of much the same standing, actually. Quite different technics, of course. Mr. Jones's work was much more abstract. Mr. Shayburn stemmed more from the impressionists."

"My," Dorian said, "there's so much I don't know about art, Mr. Bracken." There was still a phrase left over, and she decided to play the charade to the end.

"But I do know what I like," Dorian Weigand told Mr. Oscar Bracken. She watched his face. Nothing appeared on it. Not even skepticism.

In the doorway from the gallery she turned. Oscar Bracken was going back into his office.

The main floor of Bryant & Washburn was almost deserted as Dorian walked through it. The sidewalk outside was not. What appeared to be a convention jostled together at the curb and waved anxiously at buses bound downtown. Most of the buses did not stop. But there was now and then a top-lighted cab which did stop for a man or woman who had given up on the Transit Authority.

If she could work her way among the more stubborn waiters, Dorian thought, she might be lucky with a cab. She began to work her way.

It was slow going. And it was, she thought after the first jostling moments, a going of the wrong way. She should have gone up or down the avenue and taken her chance of a taxi in mid-block. Or she should have crossed the one-way avenue and waved at taxis from the other side. The two cabs which had stopped and picked passengers from the bus stop had beguiled her.

But she had already gone too far, was too enmeshed by others. And she was being jostled from behind and pushed forward toward the curb. Somebody was being inconsiderate, roughly rude. She started to turn to protest the pressing rudeness but then she was at the curb.

As she reached it a bus swerved in and, as it did, all who had been waiting for it surged forward. She held back against the pressure, but suddenly it was sharper. Somebody was pushing between her shoulder blades and the pressure was harsh, violent.

She felt herself losing balance and was in the street and the bus bearing down on her was suddenly enormous. Desperately she tried to twist her body out of its path. As she twisted she raised hands against the bus which was coming on to crush her.

She cried out, "No! *No!*" and held her hands up against the crushing bus.

XI

PROBABLY, NATHAN SHAPIRO thought, he had made one of his usual mistakes. He sat at his desk and looked moodily at the wall opposite, and considered his inadequacy–the inadequacy mysteriously not apparent to the Police Department of the City of New York. There is, he thought, more to being a detective than collecting facts and trying to fit them together. There is, finally, an ability to sense what is true and what is not true; to realize, almost by instinct, when one is being told a story which will not hold water.

There is little doubt, Shapiro thought, that Maxwell Briskie told me lies. What I should have done was to book him as a material witness and get somebody from the D.A.'s office–Bernard Simmons, preferably–and give him the full treatment. A hundred to one, Simmons, probably with Bill Weigand sitting in, would have broken down his unlikely story; got him to say, finally, "All right, I killed him."

Briskie could have said more than that and, in extenuation, probably would have said more than that. He might, for example, have contended that he had really gone to the studio to try to buy the picture his wife had posed for. He might have said there was a quarrel, and that Shackleford Jones had come at him with a gun and that they had struggled and the gun had gone off as they wrestled for it. He might have said that he went back the next day to "find" the body of his friend or to make sure his friend had really died.

Probably he had, in fact, gone back Thursday to make sure that the police would not discover something which would incriminate Maxwell Briskie. It would not be the first time a murderer had tried, after thinking things over, to return and tidy things up.

Shapiro's mistake was not irreparable. It was unlikely that

Briskie would, at least immediately, try to make a run for it. He could have the lithe little featherweight brought in and have him booked. Meanwhile . . .

Meanwhile, Shapiro looked up a telephone number and dialed it and listened to the signal of its ringing in an apartment in Gay Street. He let the signal sound half a dozen times. Rachel Farmer either was not at home or was not answering her telephone. So he could not, immediately, ask her whether, on Wednesday morning, she had met Maxwell Briskie in Little Great Smith Street—he walking away from Jones's studio and she walking, if only generally, toward it.

He looked at his watch and the hands showed a little after four. He could, if he wanted, call it a finished, if generally wasted, day. But it did not feel like a finished day. It felt like a day in which there was still something to be done, some discrepancy to be resolved.

Something in Briskie's story that didn't jibe with something else? Or something about the painting by Shackleford Jones which Dorian Weigand said had turned up in the art gallery of a Fifth Avenue store? After she had been so almost certain that Jones would not sell outright to a department store? Perhaps that was the discrepancy which nibbled in his mind—a discrepancy not in a story but in the actions of a man now dead. It might be an idea to go up to this department store gallery and find out from whoever ran it how he had got a picture by Shackleford Jones. Had Jones carried it in, possibly under his arm? Or had whoever ran the gallery gone to Jones's studio and looked around and said, "All right, I'll take that one."

If he could not be perceptive, Nathan Shapiro thought, he could at least be thorough.

He was on his feet when his telephone rang. He said, Yes, it was Lieutenant Shapiro speaking, and was asked to hold on a minute for Mr. Jeremiah Osgood. He held on a minute.

About making an appraisal of the paintings of Shackleford Jones, in behalf of Jones's widow, Mr. Osgood had had a change of mind. "Very well," Osgood said, "say she talked me into it. Appealed to my sympathies. But I felt I ought to clear it with you. And, of course, find out if the studio is sealed up, or whatever the police do under such circumstances."

It was not sealed up. It was locked up.

That, Osgood said, presented no problem. Mrs. Jones had a key.

"Tentatively," Osgood said, "I've arranged to meet her there this evening. If that will be acceptable to the police?"

Shapiro, briefly, thought it over. It might, he thought, be useful to have an expert's opinion of the value of the contents of Jones's studio. For, at the least, comparison with the expert who would eventually be appointed by the surrogate's court.

Shapiro said, "We don't object, Mr. Osgood. When is this appointment with Mrs. Jones?"

Unfortunately, Osgood was tied up and would be for some time. His tentative appointment with Mrs. Jones was for seven o'clock. The light would not be at its best so late even on a June evening. But there would be enough light for a "preliminary survey."

"I'll have a man meet you there," Shapiro said. "You can give him whatever figures you come up with, as well as giving them to Mrs. Jones."

Osgood said, "Well-l-l-l," with doubt in his voice.

"Yes," Shapiro said. "We'll do it that way, Mr. Osgood. If at all. Or, of course, you can get a court order. Mean some delay."

"Send your man along," Osgood said. "Mrs. Jones says she wants to get back home. Seems she's not partial to New York. Seven, then. The man you're sending; he know anything about paintings?"

"No," Shapiro said. "Not anything at all. As a matter of fact, I may be the man myself."

"Be glad to meet you," Osgood said, without any special conviction. "Until around seven."

He hung up with that, and Shapiro looked again at his watch. If there had been any chance of getting early back to Brooklyn, the chance was shot. He telephoned Rose and told her so, and she was resigned, if by no means happy. As he walked through the squad room he stopped at Tony Cook's desk and told Cook where to spend at least part of the evening.

Four-thirty to seven. If he was lucky with traffic, he could get to Bryant & Washburn's gallery before the store closed.

He got a cruise car to take him up, which helped with traffic, although the siren was not used at first. Then, when the car, turning back to come down Fifth Avenue above the store, came onto the avenue, it was used.

In the block below, the traffic man on duty was waving traffic toward the east side of the street. A police cruiser was parked beside a bus in front of Bryant & Washburn, and its roof light was flashing red. The driver of Shapiro's car turned on his flasher to go with his siren. A block or two uptown another siren wailed down the street. Ambulance, this time, Shapiro knew.

Shapiro's car pulled up behind the other police car and Shapiro and Sergeant Joe Friendly spilled themselves out of it.

"Break it up," a uniformed man from the first cruiser was telling a clustering crowd. "Break it up. Give the lady a chance to breathe."

Over shoulders, Shapiro saw the lady. She was Dorian Weigand. She was sitting on the curb, holding her head in her hands.

Shapiro squatted in front of Dorian and said, "Mrs. Weigand. *Mrs. Weigand.*"

Dorian took her hands from her face. Her hands were bruised. Her face was not. She said, "Where did you come from, Lieutenant? Did Bill send you?" But then she shook her head and shaking it did not seem to hurt. "I *am* shaken up," she said. "It only happened minutes ago. How could Bill . . . ?"

She moved her head again, clearing it again.

"I'm all right, really," Dorian said. "Only, somebody pushed me in front of a bus, Lieutenant."

She looked up. "That bus," she said, and pointed at it.

The bus was at the curb and the driver was out of it. He was talking to one of the policemen from the first cruise car. The driver, obviously illustrating, wrenched his hands around as if they held a steering wheel. The policeman made notes. The driver spoke loudly.

"Right out in front of me," he said. "Like she stumbled or something. Right out in *front* of me. What I thought, she was a goner. Only, she moved fast. Like–like a shortstop moves, sort of. I tell you, officer . . ."

Dorian stood up. She said, "Ouch. I certainly sat down hard." Her skirt showed she had sat down hard. But when she moved the few steps to the policeman and the driver she walked with the grace Shapiro had come to realize was part of her. And when she was near enough she held out her hand to the bus driver. He looked at it in surprise. Dorian looked at it too. It was red and already beginning to swell; two fingernails of her right hand were jaggedly broken.

"All right," she said. "The will for the deed, I guess. But I want to thank you. If you hadn't been good–very, very good–I –well, I guess I wouldn't be talking to you. Or to anybody. If you hadn't, at the last minute, turned it away from me ––"

"You were right in front of it, lady," the bus driver said. "You sure moved fast. You was lucky, lady. We was both lucky."

"Officer," Dorian said, "he couldn't have been better. As he says I–" she hesitated a minute and looked up at Shapiro, who had joined her–"I stumbled right out in front of him. It was all my fault."

"Got to make a report, all the same," the policeman said. "When we put in a call for an ambulance, we've got to make a report. You all right, lady?"

"Fine," Dorian said. "I ––"

The ambulance had finally got through traffic, its siren still wailing. A man in white came out of it and looked around and said, "Which one's hurt?" He looked at Dorian. He said, "You, miss?"

"I tried to push a bus out of the way," Dorian said. "I mean, stop it by pushing it. But I'm all right. I–what's the phrase, Lieutenant?" The last was to Shapiro.

"Declines medical attention," Shapiro said. "You're sure, Mrs. Weigand?"

She was quite sure. The patrolman would have to have her

name for his report. "Mrs. William Weigand." The patrolman said, "Seems to me–" and stopped with that.

"Yes," Shapiro said. "Captain William Weigand. Homicide, South." He identified himself, while he was about it. He also said he would take Mrs. Weigand home. In the police car, she squirmed uncomfortably and said, "I certainly did sit down hard." And then she said, "I think somebody tried to kill me, Lieutenant. I didn't stumble. Somebody pushed me."

"Tell me," Shapiro said, and threaded the car through traffic. "You're certain somebody deliberately pushed you?"

"Almost," she said. "A hard shove in the back, when I was on the curb. Just as the bus turned in toward the curb. If the driver hadn't been very good. . . ." She looked at her bruised hands. She said she had been lucky. She turned to look at the man beside her.

"No," she said. "I've no idea who it was. Or why whoever it was . . ." She paused again. "I went back to look at the picture. It isn't there any more, Lieutenant. They say it's been sold. They say it wasn't by Shack Jones but by a man named Shayburn. You see . . ."

She had told him the rest of it by the time he pulled the police car to the curb in front of the apartment house. She had begun with Myra Dedek's offer to include work of hers in a show of cartoon drawings. She would write a good report, Shapiro thought. Better than most of those it was part of his job to read. He went up to the apartment with her.

Weigand was in the apartment when they went into it. He had been standing in front of the glass which made the far wall of the living room and turned from it when he heard them and walked up the room and then said, "What's happened to you?" and spoke quickly, hurrying the words.

"I tried to push a bus around," Dorian said. "And I could do with a drink." And then she walked into the arms stretched out toward her.

Bill Weigand, who is a man for whom first things come first, made martinis for Dorian and himself, and poured a glass of sherry for Nathan Shapiro. They sat and sipped, and only after several sips did Weigand say, "All right, the two of you. Give."

He listened; now and then asked a question to clarify a point. When they had finished he said, "You can't be certain that somebody pushed you intentionally. Right?"

She said, "Right, Bill. If you mean I can't prove it, right."

"In the store," he said. "Possibly in this group in front of it. Mrs. Jones. Osgood. This curator–Bracken."

"He went back into his office when I was leaving. Of course, I took a local elevator down. It stopped at every floor."

Bill Weigand nodded his head.

"This man who works for Mrs. Dedek. Weldon ——"

Shapiro supplied the rest of the name.

"He left before I did," Dorian said. "So did Mrs. Jones. So, I suppose, did Miss Farmer. But she just happened to be in the advertising department. Looking for a job."

"A good many people just happened to be around," Weigand said. "Right? Right, Nate?"

"Yes," Shapiro said. "A good many coincidences." He finished the sherry in his small glass, and shook his head when Weigand looked at it. He sighed. He said, "Too many."

"Not including Briskie," Weigand said. "Or Mrs. Briskie. Rather a pity, isn't it, Nate? Since Briskie seems a likely client."

"Yes," Shapiro said. "We don't know the Briskies weren't there, of course. I should have put a tail on him, I suppose." He sighed. "Or have booked him."

"Has he got a key to Jones's apartment?"

"He says not. Says that the door was unlocked both times he went there. He doesn't have to be telling the truth. About any of it. But I can't, offhand, see what he'd have against Mrs. Weigand." He shook his head sadly. "There's a lot I can't see. I'm over my head. As I told ——"

"No," Weigand said. "We've had that. Right? Cook working out O.K.?"

"When I can think of something for him to do," Shapiro said. "You plan to have him go along to Jones's studio this evening?"

Shapiro did not. Detective Anthony Cook was in Gay Street, awaiting the return of Rachel Farmer, with intent to ask whether she had been in Little Great Smith Street Wednesday morning, as according to information received, she had been. And, if she had, why she hadn't mentioned it.

"You think Briskie just dragged her in? Red herring?"

That was possible, Shapiro thought. The trouble was, too damn many things were possible.

"The story he tells is possible," Shapiro said. "It doesn't, actually, sound unreasonable when you hear it. Only—there's something in it doesn't jibe with something else. The trouble is, I haven't come up with any idea what it doesn't jibe with."

Weigand assured him that he would. This did not in the least convince Lieutenant Nathan Shapiro.

While he was going down in the elevator, Shapiro realized that the glass of sherry, small as it was, had been a mistake. It had been a tangy sherry, not the kind of wine to which he was used. His stomach was talking back to him, although he had said nothing to it. Of course, it often did when Shapiro was out of his depth. Which meant most of the time.

He was in the police cruiser when he realized what, aside from the wine, was annoying his stomach. Nothing had gone into it since breakfast and that aggrieved it.

He drove the cruiser back to West Twentieth Street and turned it in to Precinct, which owned it. He had a pastrami sandwich at a counter near by and coffee to go with it. He could have done with a beer but decided his stomach couldn't. He walked, not hurrying, to the nearest Eighth Avenue subway stop and took a downtown local. He got off at West Fourth Street and began to walk west—mostly west, anyway—toward Little Great Smith Street.

He was at the intersection of West Fourth and West Twelfth streets when his mind put a tentative finger on the discrepancy which had been bothering it. Probably, of course, his memory was at fault. It often was. That could be checked out, after he had looked again at the paintings in Shackleford Jones's studio.

If, after further exposure to high colors and amazing shapes, he was still up to it.

Shapiro, with plenty of time, walked on toward (he hoped) Little Great Smith Street.

XII

SHAPIRO CLIMBED AN insecure staircase. There were no lights behind the doors of IMPERIAL NOVELTIES, INC. or PERMA-SNAPS. On each landing of the loft building an electric bulb dangled, ineffectually, from a cord. When Shapiro stood in front of the door marked "Shack" his shadow fell on the lock as he groped Rachel Farmer's studio key toward it. Finally, after some scratching around, he got the key into the lock. He then discovered he could have spared himself the groping. The door was not locked.

It was not dark in the big studio. Day still is bright at a little before seven on a June evening. But shadows gathered in the room as if shadows were holding a convention there. Shapiro found a light switch and flicked it and some of the shadows fled, but others formed in other places.

The air conditioning hummed. The police had decided to keep it in operation in case canvas and paint needed it. But, as he walked into the enormous room, feeling certain that he was alone in it, he felt a movement of air, as if a window were open somewhere.

At the end of the room, he thought. One of the two narrow windows there. Not the one with the air-conditioning unit in it. That one, almost certainly, was unopenable. The other—the one which gave access to the fire escape Briskie had used when he had been interrupted in his search for the picture of his wife?

Shapiro walked down the shadowy room, among the easels.

The window was open—wide open. He leaned out of it and looked down, and thought he saw movement near the bottom of the fire escape. But it was only movement, and he could not be sure. His right hand had moved, by reflex, toward the shoulder holster under his jacket. He moved it away from there and used it to close the window. It went down more easily than he expected and landed with a bang. And–as if that had been a signal –someone moaned.

It took him seconds to find Isabelle Jones, who lay on the floor behind a rack of paintings. He found another light switch and an overhead light went on and he crouched down beside her, and looked at the blood streaming from a head wound.

The blood came fast. At first he thought that she, like her husband, had been shot in the head. But then he could not be certain. Scalp wounds bleed freely, even when they are not deep.

She was unconscious now and not moaning. Perhaps the sound of the window's closing had, for an instant, roused her.

Shapiro found the telephone and dialed an emergency number and said what was wanted. Then he crouched again beside the unconscious woman, and used a handkerchief from his breast pocket to apply pressure to the bleeding wound. He applied it as gently as he could without making the pressure entirely ineffective.

He thought, when he could see the wound more clearly, that she had been hit savagely with what might have been a metal rod. The blow had torn the scalp. There was no telling what it had done to the skull under the scalp. That was the reason Nathan Shapiro pressed so gently. If the skull of the plump little woman from Kansas was broken he did not want to press its shards into the softness of the brain.

The handkerchief and the hand which held it grew red as Shapiro waited for the sound of sirens. It seemed a long time before he heard them. It was longer still before he heard feet on the wooden stairway.

The first footfalls were the heavy ones of a cruiser sergeant and the patrolman who teamed with him. There was a washstand in this corner of the studio loft and what appeared to be a reasonably clean hand towel hung beside it. The patrolman soaked the towel in cold water and took over from Shapiro, who went to the washstand and flushed blood off his hands and shook them dry. Then there was the sound of more feet outside and three men in white came in, one of them with a folding stretcher under his arm, and one with a black bag in his hand. The ambulance surgeon took over from the patrolman. The wound was not bleeding so freely by then. But Isabelle Jones had not stirred.

The intern from St. Vincent's counted pulsebeats. He listened to a heart. He pushed eyelids up with a gentle finger and looked into eyes which did not look back at him. He used gauze partially to clean the bleeding wound and looked at it and bandaged the battered head.

"Pulse is all right," he said. "Slight heart murmur, but she's probably always had that. Concussion. Could be a fracture. Depends on the kind of skull she's got. Need X rays for that. All right, boys."

The "boys" put the stretcher on the floor and put Isabelle Jones on the stretcher.

"Heavy one," one of the white-clad men said. "And damn steep stairs. All right, Joe?"

It was all right with Joe, and they carried the unconscious woman the length of the studio and out the studio door.

"Who is she?" the sergeant asked, and looked around the studio. His comment on it was, "Jeeze!"

Shapiro told him who the unconscious woman was. "Jones," the sergeant repeated, and then, "Wait a minute, Lieutenant. Any relation to the artist who knocked himself off?"

Shapiro answered that. He said, "You two look around and see if you can find her handbag. Big, black shiny thing, as I remember it."

It could, of course, be no more than that–could be a coincidence; could be merely that a passing burglar had come up a convenient fire escape to see what he could find, and had found a woman and slugged her–with a jimmy?–and grabbed her handbag and run for it. Possibly, Shapiro thought, when he heard me at the door, scratching around with the key.

He went to the fire-escape window and lifted it, using a pencil to press with. It went up as easily as it had gone down. Shapiro leaned out, trying to touch nothing, and examined the frame of the window. No sign it had been prized up. The window catch was not broken and not latched. All anybody would have needed to do, probably, was to push up on the window frame and the window would conveniently have popped open.

He looked at the fire-escape landing. Feet had scuffed in the sooty dust which is so major a part of the atmosphere of the city of New York. Maybe the lab boys could make more of the marks. They might even be able to guess at the size of the shoes which had made them. Perhaps they would be able to establish that two people had recently used the fire-escape landing and the iron stairs leading down from it into an areaway between this loft building and the next.

Shapiro leaned out the window and looked down. The movement he had sensed rather than seen would have been near the foot of the fire escape. Perhaps he might, after all, have fired a warning shot in that general direction, after a shouted command. He didn't, on the whole, think he should have. He might have hit something–man or woman or dog or cat. There is, to Shapiro's mind, nothing defensibly inadvertent about the use of a handgun.

"Want something, mister?" a heavy, policeman's voice said behind him and Shapiro drew back into the studio. The cruise-car sergeant was standing near the distant door, confronting a tall lean man. Shapiro said, "All right, Sergeant," and walked up the room. When he was near enough, he said, "Mr. Osgood?"

"Certainly," the tall man said. "What's going on here? I had an ——" He stopped and looked carefully at Shapiro. "Appointment," he said. "If you're Lieutenant Shapiro, with you and Mrs. Jones. Not, however, with the entire police force."

"Yes," Shapiro said, "I'm Shapiro." He looked at the watch on his wrist. "You're a bit late, Mr. Osgood. Seven the time was. It's a quarter after."

"Waited for a customer," Osgood said. "Who never showed up. What *is* this about, Lieutenant? Somebody break into Shack's studio? Or–" he shrugged his shoulders–"hasn't Mrs. Jones got here yet?"

"Got here," Shapiro said. "Been carried out of here. In Saint Vincent's Hospital by now. In the emergency ward."

Unexpectedly, Osgood said, "Goodness!"

"Come in," Shapiro said. "Find something to sit on, if you can. And–remember where you were half an hour ago."

"I don't really," Osgood said, and looked at his own watch. "I have an —"

"Come in," Shapiro said, and sounded like a policeman.

Osgood came into the studio. He took a handkerchief out and flicked the seat of a wooden chair. Then he sat on the chair.

Shapiro went to help the uniformed men find a handbag. With them he looked behind things and under things and on top of things. It took them fifteen minutes to decide they were not going to find a shiny black handbag with, presumably, Isabelle Jones's fingerprints on it.

"Maybe," the sergeant said, "she didn't have one." He considered this. "No," he said, "she'd have had one. The guy who slugged her could have grabbed it. Maybe just some small-time burglar."

"Maybe," Shapiro said. He heard more feet on the stairs. That would, probably, be a couple of men from Fingerprints. It was a couple of men from Fingerprints, and a man from the police lab.

"Somebody," Shapiro told them, "probably went out the window down there. Or in and out. Using a fire escape. Could be there were two men. You'll find my prints on one of the crossbars, incidentally. The window was open and I closed it."

He got an, "O.K., Lieutenant," from one of the men and nodded heads from the other two. He went back to Jeremiah Osgood, who did not look comfortable on the wooden chair.

"I was in a taxi on Fifth Avenue," Osgood said. "Stuck in traffic. There ought to be a law against trucks blocking the avenue at side streets. Pulling into it on a light when they know damn well the street's blocked beyond."

"There is a law," Shapiro told him. "So, half an hour ago you were in a taxi on Fifth Avenue."

"Suppose," Osgood said, "you tell me what has happened to Mrs. Jones? To put her in the hospital."

"Somebody hit her on the head. At, apparently, a little before seven. About half an hour before you got here."

"The name of the man who drove the taxi is Morris Oblonsky," Osgood said. "And I can give you his number. And, aren't they required to keep some sort of record of where they pick passengers up and let them out?"

New York hackers are required to keep such records. Passengers are not required to note the names of hackers or jot down medallion numbers. Osgood had unusual curiosity. Or was unusually foresighted.

"He was reckless," Osgood said. "I told him once or twice to take it easy. He didn't. So I wrote down his name and number. Just in case. Do you insist that I stay here, Lieutenant? I have an appointment for eight-thirty. I had expected to have time to go home and change. It's dinner and black tie."

"There are one or two points you might help us on," Shapiro said. "I don't like to inconvenience you but . . ."

Osgood would tell him what. Osgood had an apartment on West Ninth Street, which wasn't far. Unless Shapiro had to stay in the studio, why shouldn't he go to the apartment with Osgood and they could talk there? Osgood didn't know what he could tell the lieutenant, but it would be everything he could.

Shapiro considered briefly and went with him, after telling the sergeant to see that the studio was locked up when they had finished with it. Not that it seemed to do much good to lock up the studio of the late Shackleford Jones. It was a most porous studio. He got Osgood's telephone number and passed it along, as a telephone at which he could be reached if, for example, they turned up Mrs. Jones's handbag.

They were lucky with a cab, and to find a hacker who knew his way. Osgood had a studio apartment, complete with skylight, in the block on West Ninth between Fifth and Sixth, and Ninth Street turned out to be very different from Eighth. If the lieutenant would like a drink? A wave toward the bar. The lieutenant would not. If the lieutenant didn't mind they could talk between rooms while Osgood changed. It was not, to Shapiro, an ideal arrangement. It was an arrangement which he could change if he needed to.

So–how could Jeremiah Osgood help the New York police?

Help them find the murderer of a good painter, since he assumed it came to murder.

"When Mrs. Jones first asked you to appraise Jones's work," Shapiro said, his voice raised to reach the bedroom in which Osgood was changing, "you agreed to. Then you said–on your lawyer's advice–you had changed your mind. Then you changed it again. Why?"

"Talked to my lawyer when it appeared to be getting complicated. Followed his advice. Then Mrs. Jones called again and told me about this list. You know about that, I assume?"

Osgood came to the door of the living room, suspenders dangling from dark blue dress trousers.

"No," Shapiro said.

"Assumed you'd come across the original in his papers," Osgood said. "What she has, she says, is a carbon. I haven't seen it. She was to bring it along this evening and ––" He stopped abruptly. Then he said, "That handbag you were all looking for?"

"If she brought a list to show you, I'd assume she brought it in her bag," Shapiro said. "A list of what?"

Osgood said, "Minute," from the bedroom. It was a little more than that. He came back with suspenders up and black tie on and a cummerbund around a trim waist. He carried a deep blue dinner jacket. In the living room he put it on, and was ready for a black-tie dinner.

"Of paintings, I suppose," Osgood said. "Titles and dates, at any rate. About thirty, she says. Sure you won't have a drink?"

Shapiro was sure he wouldn't have a drink. Osgood poured scotch into a glass and added water and a single cube of ice. He came back and sat down facing the dark-haired, sad-faced lieutenant of detectives. When he talked, between sips from his glass, he talked with unexpected succinctness. He could, of course, pass on only what Mrs. Jones had told him.

Between two and three weeks before she had got in the mail, with a New York postmark, a two-page typed list of titles and dates. It had been a carbon. With the typed sheets, but in longhand, in pencil on typewriter paper, a brief message beginning, "Hi," and signed "Shack." She could quote the message, and had to Osgood. The message was: "Stick these in Papa's safe for me, will you? Could be I'll need them." That was all. She had done what she was asked to do. "I could never make any sense out of him, anyway," she had told Osgood–he said, sipping his drink, she had told him.

She had telephoned her father the evening she got to New York. He had got the list out of his safe and mailed it to her airmail, special delivery.

"She got it this afternoon," Osgood said. "Got me on the telephone and told me about it. And–well, I got interested, Lieutenant. All my lawyer had said was that, if he were in my place, he'd stay out of it. I decided it wouldn't do any harm to have a look at the list. And see the pictures which went with it."

"She hadn't any idea why he had sent her the list?"

Osgood had passed on all he had been told by Isabelle Jones.

Would it be a usual thing for a painter to make a list of his paintings? Or, if there were only thirty titles on the list Jones had sent his wife, a partial list? Because, at a guess, there must be upwards of a hundred canvases, large and small, in Jones's large studio.

Osgood, a little elaborately, shrugged his shoulders.

"Never know what one of them may do," he said. "Take one, and he's sensible and businesslike. Take another and you'd swear he was nuts. From what little I know of Jones I'd say he was–call it eccentric."

He regarded his glass.

"There's this," he said. "Most of them, probably, would make a list of pictures they had chosen for an exhibit. Before they shipped them off, or the gallery sent somebody to collect them." He smiled faintly at his glass. "A good many of them," he said, "are suspicious of dealers. Think we're out to do them in. Ours isn't, what with one thing and another, a restful occupation."

"Would they have titles for their paintings?"

"You mean on them? As a writer puts a title on a story? No. In their minds, Yes, I suppose so. Descriptions in their minds. Of course, they generalize. 'Composition,' or 'Composition in

Yellow.' Or 'Still Life With Flowers.' Descriptions which might apply to a hundred paintings by as many painters."

"So the list, even if we had it, wouldn't ——"

But Shapiro stopped, because Osgood was shaking his head. He completed the head shaking with the word, "No."

"With dates," he said, "and most of them date. With even a general description, a man familiar with an artist's work could pretty well tell what the painter had had in mind. Even a painter as modern as Shack was."

"You mean an expert could?"

He could call it that.

"If you had a copy of this list which Mrs. Jones probably has lost, if she's lost her handbag, you'd be able to pick out the paintings he'd made the list of?"

"I think so. For the most part, at any rate. Of course, if he just called a painting, say, 'Still Life,' and gave a dating year for it, and there were several others in the same year all called 'Still Life'–well, nobody could know which one he had in mind. But maybe he'd describe one as–oh, 'Still Life With Pitcher.' That would help, of course. Or, as I said, 'With Flowers.'"

"You could tell, in Mr. Jones's work, which was a pitcher, and which were flowers?"

Shapiro spoke with doubt. Osgood laughed, and saw what Shapiro meant. He said, "Probably," and added, "For the most part." And he looked at his watch and then at Shapiro with raised eyebrows. He said, "The dinner's on Park in the Nineties, Lieutenant. If there's more, couldn't we ——"

The telephone interrupted him and he walked the living room to answer it. He looked very much as a man going to a black-tie dinner on Park Avenue should look, or Shapiro supposed he did.

"A Detective Flanagan. Says he's at Saint Vincent's."

Shapiro went to the telephone looking, he supposed, like a tired detective in a gray summer suit which, after a day as warm as this had been, undoubtedly needed pressing.

Mrs. Shackleford Jones had recovered consciousness. The physician attending her said she could be talked to.

It is an easy walk from West Ninth Street near Sixth to St.

Vincent's Hospital, between Eleventh and Twelfth streets on Seventh. Mrs. Jones was in a private room on the third floor of one of the older wings. Detective Michael Flanagan was sitting on a straight chair outside the door. He plopped the chair down to four legs and stood up. He said that, from what they said, it was all right to go on in.

Mrs. Jones looked even plumper in a hospital bed than she did out of it. Her head was extensively bandaged. But there was nothing wrong with her voice when she said, "So it's you, is it? A lot of care you take of people here in New York. I might have been killed, for all you did about it."

"I was there at a little before seven," Shapiro said. "Before the time you and Mr. Osgood had set."

"So I was ahead of time," Mrs. Jones said. "It's my late husband's place, isn't it? I'd a right to be protected, hadn't I? The way you people do things in this city you make so much of!"

Shapiro said he was very sorry. He said, "Suppose you tell me what happened, Mrs. Jones?"

She had let herself in with her key. There had been nobody there. Nobody she saw, anyway. She realized now, of course, that there had been somebody lurking there. Hiding behind something. It had got so a person wasn't safe anywhere in New York. All those muggings.

Shapiro was patient. He said, "You had a list with you, I understand."

"Of course I had a list. The one he sent me."

"And you and Mr. Osgood planned to try to identify the pictures on the list. Your husband had given you no explanation of why he sent you the list?"

"You seem to know all about it," she said. "It was the way he was. Irresponsible. Years ago I found out what kind of man he was."

"You started to try to identify the pictures without waiting for Mr. Osgood to get there?"

She had.

"No order about any of it," she said. "Just higgledy-piggledy. Also, the place needed a good cleaning. If Papa ran his store like that." She started to shake her head and stopped that and said, "Ouch! These city doctors. Makes a person wonder if they know what they're doing."

"This is a good hospital," Shapiro told her.

She said, "Huh!"

Shapiro's patience held. It led him to statements from which he managed to strip the verbal fringe.

She had at first looked at the pictures nearest the door. None of them seemed to fit the descriptions on the list. But how on earth was a person to tell? She had worked her way back into the depths of the studio. There were racks there, and she had begun to take paintings out of the racks.

She had heard someone behind her and had said something, assuming the person she heard was Jeremiah Osgood. "Took you long enough to get here," was what she remembered she had said. Then there was something like a big flash, and the next thing she knew she was here in this place.

"This sound you heard," Shapiro said. "Somebody walking behind you?"

She thought so. It was all "knocked out of her head." And no wonder.

"Could you have heard a window opening? Could that have been the sound? Or that and then somebody walking on the floor?"

She thought just somebody walking.

Heavy footsteps, as of a man? Or the lighter, sharper, footfalls of a woman?

"What you mean is," she told him, "whoever it was got away. That's what you mean, isn't it?"

He was afraid so. This list, she had carried it in her handbag? Taking it out now and then to look at it? Check a listing against a picture?

Of course. What did he think? And why didn't he just look in her handbag and find out. But then she said, "Oh!"

"Yes," Shapiro said, "I'm afraid your handbag is missing, Mrs. Jones."

She said, "What I would have expected. Just what I would have expected in a city like this."

There was more about the city like that, with considerable reference to the superiority of folkways in Emporia, Kansas. Of police-ways in particular.

Shapiro's patience held. He guided her back to what he wanted to know. Could she remember any of the titles, or descriptions if they were not titles, on the list? And any of the dates?

The titles, descriptions–whatever they were–hadn't meant anything. "Any more than what he called his paintings did." She did remember one, anyway. "Composition With Figures." It had been dated the previous year. And there were several others listed merely as "Composition," with dates. No, she did not remember that more than one painting so described had been dated in the same year. And what had he meant by "Composition"? It didn't tell a person anything about what a picture was about, did it?

"They tell me that pictures aren't necessarily *about* anything," Shapiro said. "I don't know what they mean, precisely."

"You and me."

"As for composition, I suppose it's an arrangement of shapes in a certain way. In balance, perhaps." He remembered some of Shackleford Jones's paintings. "Or out of it," he added.

"Arrangements," she repeated. "Like flower arrangements?"

Shapiro didn't know. Perhaps, in a sense.

"We do those at the garden club," Mrs. Jones said. "He listed several things he called just 'Still Life.' And–I do remember this –one called 'Reclining Figure.' Probably a woman with no clothes on. He was always after me to pose that way. When we were first married. I had a good figure. That I'll say for myself."

"Did you pose?" Shapiro asked, and realized that, as usual, curiosity was leading into a dead-end street.

"Certainly not," she said. "What do you think I was?"

A man's wife, Shapiro thought, but did not say. Did she happen to remember a listing for a picture called "Cityscape?" What he could see of her face amid the bandages took on a puzzled expression, or he thought it did. She said, "Like fire escape?"

"More," Shapiro said, "like 'landscape.'"

"No," she said. "I don't remember anything like that. 'Landscape.' Yes, I think there was one called that. The date on it was –oh, three or four years ago. No, wait. It was 'Landscape With Cat.' Whatever that means. And there was something called 'The Melting Clown.' I tell you, the man wasn't in his right mind. He never was, really. Not being good enough to get a job with the greeting card company did something to him, I always thought."

And probably, Shapiro guessed, always said. He felt a passing sympathy for the late Shackleford Jones.

"I remember one other," Isabelle Jones said. "It didn't make any sense any more than the others did. Something called 'Urban Rectangles.' It was dated last year, I think. I mean, just the year. He was always vague about things like that."

She did not remember any other descriptions or titles from the list. She did remember how many paintings had been listed. If, of course, the list she had been sent was one of paintings. There had been thirty-two. She had counted.

"Mr. Osgood said you plan to go back home," Shapiro said. "We'd a little rather ––"

"Well," she said, "I'm not going. Nobody's going to scare me out of here until I find out what's going on. You can bet on that, Lieutenant. Not that I won't be glad to get out of this terrible city."

From a booth on the main floor, Shapiro dialed the number of the Weigand apartment. He got no answer.

XIII

DETECTIVE ANTHONY COOK told Lieutenant Nathan Shapiro that the Farmer dame was quite a dame. And that she had been in Little Great Smith Street on Wednesday morning and that she had seen Maxwell Briskie there and that she was certainly not on her way to Shack Jones's studio and that she considered Briskie a louse, trying to drag her into it when he was in it himself up to the ears, and that she hadn't mentioned being there because nobody had asked her. And because she had thought Maxie was a friend of hers. The louse.

She had opened her apartment door to Cook only to the extent of the guard chain and looked at him and said, "Now what, for God's sake?" She had added that she was tired of being badgered by cops. But then she had looked at Cook more carefully and said, "All right. Come on in."

She had been wearing a robe which, as she moved ahead of Cook into the living room and then turned to face him, only intermittently covered her long, slender body. Cook resolutely remembered he was a detective, on duty. And she had laughed at him and then had said, "Anyway, I guess you're not one of the gay boys. Makes a nice change. What do you want, mister?" She laughed again. "Among other things," she said.

Cook brought his mind back from its rather pleasant wandering.

"To know where you were Wednesday morning," Cook said. "At about ten o'clock, Miss Farmer." The "Miss Farmer" was to steady things.

She sat down in a low chair and crossed long legs.

("Regardless," Cook told Shapiro, across Shapiro's desk in the offices of Homicide, Manhattan South. Shapiro said he had met Miss Rachel Farmer.)

"Walking along Little Great Smith Street," Rachel Farmer had told Cook. "About a block from Shack's studio. I suppose Maxie passed the word along? He's a louse, isn't he?"

Cook reserved comment. He said, "Going to Mr. Jones's studio, Miss Farmer?"

"I certainly was not. Did Maxie say I was? Trying to drag me into something to save his own hide. Do you want a drink? Because I do."

Cook said he did not want a drink, which was not strictly true. "Where were you going, Miss Farmer?"

Rachel Farmer swirled out of the low chair, her silk robe swirling with her, at an indiscreet distance. She walked across the room and banged with a small fist against wood paneling. A section of the panel opened and Rachel reached into a cupboard and came out with a long-necked bottle. She poured what Cook took to be wine into a small glass and returned to the chair she had been sitting in. She swirled back into the chair and crossed long bare legs.

("Regardless," Cook said. "Yes," Shapiro said, "I got the point before, Tony.")

"Where were you going, Miss Farmer?" Cook asked again, in as much a cop's voice as circumstances permitted.

"To pose for Malcolm Serbin," Rachel said. "You know his work, I expect? All coils, sort of. Except when he's being an illustrator. He's doing a nude coming out of the ocean. For a fish company."

It was warm in the living room, among other things. Cook wiped his forehead with a handkerchief.

"Take your jacket off if you want to," Rachel told him. "Or aren't you supposed to expose your revolver?"

("Kidding, sort of," Cook told Shapiro. "As if we were playing games. What do you suppose she meant, 'a fish company'?" "I don't know, Tony. About Wednesday morning?")

She was there. She'd walked from Gay Street and was supposed to be at this Serbin's place at ten. And about a block from Shackleford Jones's studio she had run into Maxwell Briskie.

"You didn't tell us this before. Why?"

"Because you didn't ask me, mister. And because it didn't

have anything to do with anything." She paused then, and sipped from her small glass. She said, "Come to think of it, maybe it did." She put the glass down on a small table. She said, "I've always liked Maxie, mister. I didn't want to drag him into something. But if he wants it the other way round." She picked the glass up again and sipped from it.

"All right," she said, "he looked to me like he'd been in a fight with somebody. And that somebody had hit him on the side of the face. And he was walking fast. Almost running, I guess. He said, 'Hi,' and I said, 'Hi, Maxie. Thought you were in —' But he kept on going."

"Thought he was in what, Miss Farmer?"

"Chicago. The night before he had said he was flying out there. Something about a mural he was maybe going to do."

"A bruise on his face? Or a cut?"

It had been just a bruise, she thought. On the left side of his face, below the cheekbone. It had been "sort of blackish-purplish."

"Of course," she said, "he's a great one for going to gyms. He used to be a boxer, he says. Pretty good, to hear him tell it. For all he's pint-size. Maybe he was boxing in a gym and somebody punched him."

"You didn't see where he came from? I mean—out of a building somewhere?"

She had not. But, yes, he was coming from the direction of the loft building in which Shack Jones had a studio.

Cook had taken the address and telephone number of Malcolm Serbin, who had been doing a picture of a nude coming out of the ocean. For a fish company. After he had left Rachel Farmer's apartment, and climbed a flight of stairs and knocked on the apartment door of Mr. and Mrs. Maxwell Briskie and got no answer, Cook had found a telephone booth. He had dialed the number Rachel had given him and Serbin had answered his telephone.

Rachel Farmer had posed for him Wednesday morning. Yes, he thought she had got there somewhere around ten. Stayed a couple of hours. At ten dollars an hour.

"Around ten?"

She hadn't punched a time clock, if that was what Detective Cook was getting at. Near enough to ten.

"That's about it," Cook said. He looked at his watch. He said, "Want I should type it out tonight, Lieutenant? Because I haven't had dinner and—well, I've sort of got a date."

Morning would be time enough for the formal report, Shapiro told Detective Anthony Cook.

"Could be I'll be down that way later," Cook said. "Off-duty. Shall I have another shot at getting Briskie's side of it?"

"If you happen to be down that way."

"There's an Italian restaurant around there I go to sometimes," Cook said. "Good lasagna."

What a detective does when off duty is a detective's business, providing he does nothing illegal and carries his gun. There is nothing illegal about eating lasagna. Cook was a youngish man and probably had a good digestion. Nathan Shapiro sighed and regarded the top of his desk, and thought of going home.

But something fidgeted beneath the surface of that pleasant thought. Shapiro tried to probe beneath the surface. Probably, he thought, the discrepancy he fumbled for would stick out a mile to anybody else. Perhaps something about the picture which wasn't by Shackleford Jones, but by a painter named Alan Shayburn, which had been called "Cityscape" and which no longer hung in the art gallery of Bryant & Washburn? Shapiro puzzled over it. There was something . . .

Of course. And nothing much. "Urban Rectangles" and "Cityscape" might conceivably be different titles for the same picture. And obviously might not. Pictures are not "about" anything. He had, Shapiro thought, learned that, if little else.

Probably the itching in his mind was not caused by the painting, which had been sold to somebody. It concerned something he had been told. He fumbled further. He began to feel that it was something he had been told by Maxwell Briskie, who had had a bruised face when he walked through Little Great Smith Street on Wednesday morning. Who had, further, gone back to Jones's studio the next day.

Shapiro searched his mind for the precise details of Briskie's story of the two days, and found them, neatly filed. For, of course, what they were worth. There remained something which did not jibe with something else. He looked up the report Detective James O'Brien, of Precinct, had made concerning his brief interview with Myra Dedek when she was still in shock because of what she had walked in on. Shapiro tried to match things which wouldn't match.

He dialed the telephone number of Maxwell Briskie and let the telephone in Gay Street ring four times. He was about to give it up when Briskie answered. He was panting slightly. He said, "Hold it a minute, will you?" and Shapiro held it. "Had to run upstairs," Briskie said. "Wind isn't what it used to be. Who did you say?"

Shapiro repeated his name. He got "Oh," for an answer, the inflection trailing down. Briskie was, Shapiro thought, disappointed.

"Small point we'd like to clarify," Shapiro said. "You be around for, say, half an hour or so?"

He was asked what was the matter with the telephone.

"Rather see you, if it's all the same with you," Shapiro said. "Shouldn't take more than a few minutes." He waited a second. "Unless," he said, "you'd rather come here. To West Twentieth."

"Come along," Briskie said. "Bringing your small point."

Shapiro went downtown by subway. Gay Street was no longer difficult to find. As he turned at the jog in the middle of its block he saw a couple walking away from him toward Waverly Place. Rachel Farmer was almost, but not quite, as tall as Detective Anthony Cook, who was a youngish man with a good digestion. And who was not doing anything illegal. At the moment, anyway.

Briskie had, Shapiro thought, been near the button in the hallway of his apartment. The lock release in the vestibule of the building buzzed admission while Shapiro's finger was still on the doorbell. Briskie was waiting for him on the stair landing. He looked at Shapiro intently. He said, "Don't see the rubber hose, Lieutenant."

"Left it uptown," Shapiro told him, and followed him into the apartment. It was well lighted. It was Shapiro's turn to look intently. No bruise he could see on Maxwell Briskie's face. Perhaps Briskie healed quickly. Perhaps he was using some preparation which would cover a bruise. Shapiro didn't think so.

He told Briskie what Rachel Farmer had said about him.

"Up to tricks again, Rache is," Briskie said. "Full of tricks, the girl is. And sore because I'd squealed on her. See any signs of a bruise, Lieutenant?"

He sat down, quickly, in a chair with a reading light beside it. He tilted his head so that the light fell on his left cheek. Shapiro looked at the face.

"Now and then," Briskie said, "the lady's a malicious bitch. Mostly she's just scatterbrained. Well?"

There wasn't any bruise, or the remnants of a bruise.

"Why would she lie about it?" Shapiro asked.

"Fun and games," Briskie said. "Getting her own back. Perhaps, to give her the benefit of the doubt, there was something like ——"

He stopped and looked thoughtfully at nothing in particular. After a moment, he said he would be damned. Then he said, "I slandered the lady, Lieutenant. Next time I see her I'll take her flowers."

"Yes?"

"I see why the telephone wouldn't do," Briskie said. "Wanted to see for yourself."

"Yes. That came into it."

"All right. She did see something. Could have, anyway. A smudge, not a bruise. Shack wasn't a very good housekeeper, poor devil. What happened, apparently, I put my hand on something there Wednesday and then put the hand against my face. And left a hell of a smudge. I didn't know it until I got back to my own studio and looked in the mirror. So I washed my face. All there was to it. Innocent mistake."

"Clears it up," Shapiro said.

"You thought I'd been in a fight with Shack? And that he'd slugged me?"

"It seemed possible."

"And I grabbed his gun? He did keep it lying around loose. To show what a tough character he was, I always thought."

"Was he?"

"He could be, I guess. It was more–oh, he had an image of himself. The he-man type. Hundred per cent virile. You know the kind?"

"Yes," Shapiro said. "I've run into them. You doubt he was?"

"No, I don't particularly. If you mean overcompensating. Protesting too much. But I'm not his analyst."

"He went to an analyst?"

"Sure," Briskie said. "Doesn't everybody?"

"No," Shapiro said. "Do you, by the way?"

"Is it any of your business?"

"None."

"In that case, no, I don't. When I found out I wasn't going to be as tall as most men, and I did when I was in high school, I didn't need to ask an analyst what to do. I learned to box. And I came damn near making the Olympic team as a featherweight." He smiled suddenly, widely, and came up out of the chair. "Want to try me out?" he asked Shapiro.

Shapiro shook his head.

"If I had had a tussle with Shack, he wouldn't have touched me," Briskie said.

"All right. He wouldn't have touched you."

"So. Satisfied, Lieutenant?"

"For now," Shapiro said, and that there was one other small point. Would Mr. Briskie mind telling again, as precisely as he could remember, what happened in Shackleford Jones's studio when he went there and found Jones's body?

"Think you'll catch me out about something?"

"Let's say I want to refresh my memory," Shapiro said. "Of course, I can still take you in and ask you to make a formal statement. And you can call your lawyer. If you want to waste our time."

"I went, complete with check, to pick up a picture. I . . ."

He told the story as he had told it before. Not word for

word, as if he had committed his story to memory. That happened sometimes. It was always worth looking for.

Shapiro's memory had, somewhat to his surprise, been entirely accurate. And the discrepancy remained. Perhaps it did not stick out a mile and perhaps it was not important. But it was there. Nathan Shapiro turned it over in his mind on his way home to Brooklyn. Of course, no two people see or hear things in precisely the same way, including events in which they are personally involved. Even when they intend accurate reports. A policeman is used to getting disparate accounts from witnesses who should have seen the same things happen. This is one of the trials of a policeman's lot.

When Shapiro got home, Rose had long since walked the dog.

There is a kind of emptiness about the city of New York on Saturday mornings in the summer. People who go into it from out of town do not equal in numbers those who leave it for the country, or for the beaches. And most of those who remain in the city sleep late, since on Saturdays most time clocks do not tick. It is even possible to get a seat in the subway during the hour between eight and nine in the morning. Shapiro got one on a train from Brooklyn. Anthony Cook got one on a train down from the Bronx.

"Get anything useful from Miss Farmer?" Shapiro asked Cook, in the squad room of Homicide, Manhattan South. It is suitable that a lieutenant of detectives appear omniscient. Cook looked at him with surprise. "Lasagna," Shapiro said.

"She seems like an all right kid," Cook said. "Sort of nuts, but all right. Comes from California, originally. Wants to be a fashion designer. Being a model is just filling in and making a living. Says she was surprised as hell when Jones called her up a couple of weeks ago and wanted her to pose, because everybody thought he was in Spain or somewhere. Says she was even more surprised when she went around and found out he had shaved off his beard. Because it was a sort of trademark, and had been for years. Anyway, that was what she'd heard. He'd walk along the street and everybody would look at him, and if they didn't know who he was they'd ask, and that he liked. She said, 'Of course, a lot of them are sort of crazy. Egomaniacs.' But that Shack wasn't any worse than a lot of them, except that he shouted a lot. And that he was the last man she would have thought would kill himself. All right, Lieutenant, how did you know?"

"Saw you," Shapiro said. "On your way to this Italian restaurant you're fond of, I supposed. Briskie says his face was dirty. Not bruised. And, Tony, she wasn't far from Jones's studio Wednesday morning."

"I think she's an all right kid," Cook said. "And, I'm watching my step."

He was at his desk. He had been typing when Shapiro walked into the squad room. He looked up at Shapiro.

"O.K.," Shapiro said. "Didn't question it, Tony. When you get the report done, I want you to ring some doorbells."

It was not precisely that. That was merely a phrase for it–for the slow, slogging routine which is most of police work. What Detective Anthony Cook was to do was to get a list of stores which had art galleries and find out whether any of them had for sale paintings by Shackleford Jones. Or had been offered any. And, if offered any, by whom. And whether any of the clerks or curators, or whatever they called themselves, had known Jones. And if they had, whether, in the past few weeks, they had seen him in their galleries.

Cook said, "Will do." Then he said, "Want to know any more about last night, Lieutenant?"

Shapiro said, "No," and went to the cubbyhole which was his office.

He used his telephone. Oscar Bracken would be at the Bryant & Washburn gallery until noon. He took Saturday afternoons off. If it was about that painting somebody had thought was by Shackleford Jones, the police would be wasting their time. But if they wanted to waste it, that was up to them.

Bracken, Shapiro thought, was quick at putting two and two together. He said there were a couple of small points, and that he'd be along well before noon.

He used his telephone again. Except for swollen hands, Dorian

Weigand was fine. Yes, "Urban Rectangles" would be as good a title for the painting she had seen at Bryant & Washburn's as "Cityscape." No, nothing she had seen at Jones's studio looked like a picture which might be called "The Melting Clown." But putting titles on pictures ——

"I know," Shapiro said. "Pictures aren't about anything."

Was she now as convinced as she had been yesterday that the painting called "Cityscape" was by Shackleford Jones?

"Yes," she said. "From the whole feel of it. And when I saw it I was—oh, pretty well up on the style of Shack Jones. With the way he laid on paint. With everything about what he did. But ——" She hesitated. "I'm not an expert; couldn't conceivably qualify as one. And Mr. Bracken says the painting was by a man named Shayburn. Who's dead, as I told you. And Myra is certain Jones wouldn't have sold to a store and that, anyway, the picture I described doesn't feel like a Shack."

"But you'd stick to your opinion?"

"For what it's worth. As I'm saying, it isn't worth much. It's—oh, more of a feeling than an opinion. Based on intangibles. Arrived at subjectively. Nobody would listen, Lieutenant. Probably Mr. Bracken could produce something entirely tangible. A bill of sale, or something like that. Is it important?"

"I don't know, Mrs. Weigand. I'm trying to find out. You think Mr. Bracken recognized you yesterday?"

She could not be sure. She thought so. From the time he had been a partner of Myra Dedek's when there had been an exhibit, in a group, of sketches by Dorian Hunt.

A partner?

She thought so, or that it came to that. It had, as she remembered from several years back, had the feel of that. Although, she was almost certain, it had been the "Myra Dedek Galleries." Not "Dedek and Bracken," or anything like that.

"There was a feeling of authority," she said. "I'm a great one for feelings this morning, aren't I, Lieutenant? Perhaps he was just a clerk. Like this Weldon Williams, who's there now. As I remember it, it didn't feel like that, then. But—warmed over intuition, isn't it? And so no real help. Bill will be disappointed in me."

"No," Shapiro said. "But don't walk in front of buses, Mrs. Weigand."

"Today," Dorian said, "I stick to taxicabs."

People get notions, Oscar Bracken told Shapiro, and sighed over the notions people get. He also mentioned that a little learning is a dangerous thing. Not that, in her own field, Dorian Hunt was not professional. But hers was entirely another field. The painting she had been so sure was by Shackleford Jones did not, actually, in any significant way resemble the work of Shackleford Jones. Entirely different in style, in composition. In brushwork, come to that.

"You did recognize Miss Hunt? That is, Mrs. Weigand?"

Oscar Bracken, who was tall and lean and somewhere in his forties, was formally dressed. Shapiro rather felt that he should be wearing a flower in his buttonhole. He leaned back in the chair behind his desk in his small, very modern, office off the art gallery of Bryant & Washburn's furniture department.

"Not when she was here first," he said. "Then she seemed only vaguely familiar. I had only a feeling I had seen her somewhere before. When she came back, with this—er—pretense that she wanted to buy the picture—yes, then I did recognize her. But I—er—assumed that she had some reason for not wanting me to."

He tilted forward in his chair.

"What is all this, Lieutenant?" he said. "A woman—one who isn't an expert in such things—makes a mistake about a picture. I realize, of course, that being the wife of a police captain gives her a—oh, a certain credibility. Among the police, at any rate. That she has to be listened to. Are you implying that I lied to her? That I'm lying to you? Why on earth would I? We never had a Shack here. Were never offered one."

"A man dies under suspicious circumstances," Shapiro said. "There is a chance that he has been killed. We have to poke into all sorts of things. Mrs. Dedek—you know her, I gather?"

"I was associated with her at one time."

"Mrs. Dedek seems to be quite sure that Mr. Jones would not have sold his paintings to stores. Mrs. Weigand was quite sure that the painting you had here for sale was one of his. Apparently she was wrong. But it's the sort of thing we have to go into. Check out. Something that doesn't fit into what appears to be a pattern."

Bracken shook his head.

"Put it in another way," Shapiro said, with the feeling that he was making speeches. "Five days a week a man takes a certain train from New York to his home in the suburbs. Say he takes a five-oh-two train. But one day he takes a train which leaves an hour later. And that day he dies suddenly, violently. Probably the train he took has nothing to do with it. But—it was a break in his routine. Why did he change his routine? See what I mean, Mr. Bracken?"

Bracken supposed so. The police had to satisfy themselves about even the most trivial things. He hoped the lieutenant now was satisfied about this Shayburn picture.

"I understand," Shapiro said, "that Mr. Shayburn is dead?"

"A great pity," Bracken said. "He had considerable promise. He was quite a young man. Yes, he died almost a year ago."

"The store has, I suppose, some record of his sale to you? A bill of sale? Something of the sort?"

The accounting department of course had. Unfortunately, the accounting department was closed on Saturdays.

Would the records describe the picture? Identify it?

"I'm getting a little tired of this," Bracken said. "You still seem to doubt what I've told you."

"No," Shapiro said. "It's only that we have to do things in a certain way, according to rules. I've got to report to my superiors, Mr. Bracken. It isn't what *I* think. I go to the inspector and tell him this picture wasn't by Jones—not that it's likely to come up, but suppose it does—and he says, 'Can this man Bracken prove that?' And I say, 'Sorry, sir, but I didn't think to go into that.' And he says, 'You're going back into uniform, Patrolman Shapiro. To a beat in Staten Island. Maybe you'll learn to think.'"

Shapiro could imagine few less likely conversations. But he was not yet ready for Oscar Bracken to get tired into silence.

"Monday," Bracken said. "Go to accounting Monday and you'll get all the proof you want."

Shapiro said he didn't doubt it. Nor did he doubt it. He was quite sure that, on a given date in the past, Bryant & Washburn had purchased a painting from a man named Alan Shayburn. He doubted whether the records would include a photograph of the painting.

He moved as if he were about to get up; spoke as if something altogether trivial had just passed across his mind.

"You say," he said, "that you and Mrs. Dedek were once associated. Partners? Was that it?"

"What on earth?"

"Just getting things as straight as I can," Shapiro said. "Strange new world to me, Mr. Bracken. You were?"

"For a couple of years," Bracken said. "I had a small gallery of my own. We—call it merged. Running a gallery can be an expensive business, Lieutenant. Something artists never seem to understand."

"You dissolved the partnership?"

"A year or so ago, I was approached to start the gallery here. And—I don't see that this has anything to do with what you're after, but since you're curious—Myra and I weren't doing especially well financially. Overhead ate things up. It's a chancy business, dealing in art. Particularly when you want to do it on a grand scale, as Myra does. In your own building."

"She owns the building?"

"Has an equity, anyway. Actually, it was her insistence on buying instead of renting that we broke up on. I'm—well, past the age when I want to take a flyer. You're going rather far afield, aren't you?"

"One thing does seem to lead to another," Shapiro said, and spoke in a tone of mild apology. "I suppose you knew Mr. Jones? When you were associated with Mrs. Dedek."

"Not well," Bracken said. "Myra was already handling him when I joined up with her. Kept on doing it. I knew him to speak to, of course. To speak to, usually, about the prices he wanted us to hold out for. Out of line, some of them were."

"He was difficult to deal with?"

"All artists are difficult to deal with, Lieutenant," Oscar Bracken said, and made a gesture with both hands to indicate the problems presented by artists. "All the moderns are Picassos, to hear them talk. All dealers are out to do them in. A very abused lot, artists."

"Mr. Jones more than most?"

"No, I wouldn't say so. More flamboyant than most, maybe. That beard of his!"

"I've heard about the beard," Shapiro said. "Something of a trademark of his, I gather. At any rate, before beards got to be such a thing. You couldn't miss it, I gather."

"You certainly couldn't. Which was his idea, I always thought."

Shapiro stood up, and had another afterthought.

"By the way," he said, "was Mr. Jones in the gallery here recently? Past few weeks?"

"No," Bracken said. "Never was here, so far as I know. Certainly not when I was around. And if somebody else had been helping customers, he would have mentioned Shack Jones if he'd seen him. Sort of man who got himself mentioned."

"And recognized," Shapiro said. "Because of his curly, reddish beard."

"Yes," Bracken said. "It was quite a beard."

Shapiro gathered as much. And he rather wished he had seen it. And he was sorry he had taken up so much of Mr. Bracken's time.

At the door he had another afterthought. He understood that Weldon Williams, Mrs. Dedek's assistant, had been in to see Mr. Bracken the day before. Would Mr. Bracken mind telling him why?

Bracken couldn't see that it was any business of the police. Shapiro shrugged his shoulders. But if the lieutenant thought it was ——

"To see if he could get taken on here for the summer," Bracken said. "As an assistant in the gallery. Mrs. Dedek closes up for

July and August. Most of them do. Some of them around the middle of June. People don't buy pictures in the summer."

"Did he get the job?"

"Told him to try Personnel," Bracken said. "But I've told Personnel we don't need him. People don't buy many pictures from us in the summer, either."

XIV

DETECTIVE ANTHONY COOK finished his report and separated ribbon copy from carbons–the ribbon for the Deputy Chief Inspector, Commanding, Detective Division–and put them in a basket for collection by the probationary patrolman who was acting as clerk for the squad. He got from Detective Michael Corrigan the name of the man Corrigan knew in the art department of the New York *Times* and from him a list of stores which operated art galleries in connection with furniture displays. There were seven stores on the list, dotted uptown from Thirty-third Street. He was getting up from his desk to start a round of doorbell-ringing when his own telephone rang. He identified himself.

"'Morning, mister," Rachel Farmer said. "It was very good lasagna. We must have it again."

Her voice was much softer on the telephone than when one spoke to her face to face. There was a kind of coo in her voice on the telephone.

Cook kept any responsive coo out of his voice. Off-duty hours were one thing. He said, "Good morning, Miss Farmer." But he sat down again at his desk.

"I suppose you're busy," Rachel said. "Chasing people. No time for girl friends."

"Well," Cook said, "I am on duty, Miss Farmer."

"Forgive me for living, mister."

"Well . . ." Cook said. *Well* is always a useful word to bridge with. "This is an official telephone, Miss Farmer. I'm going on a job. Perhaps I could call back from ——"

"I won't be here. I'm a working girl. Got to be shouted at by painters, mister."

"Do you have to call me mister?"

"I call everybody mister. Unless I call them sister, of course. Although sometimes it's hard to tell the difference, isn't it? Tuesday, he mumbled a lot. I just remembered after you left. He was terribly grumpy about something. Of course, he usually mumbled a lot when he was working. Took his mind off what he was doing, I always thought."

Cook pulled himself together as well as he could manage.

"Which mister are you talking about, Miss Farmer?"

"Shack Jones of course," she said, tempering her tone to a shorn mind. "Tuesday. The day before he was supposed to have shot himself. He was in a thing when I was posing for him. Fuming. Talking to himself, really. Once I thought he was maybe talking to me, too, and I said, 'What, mister?' And he said, 'Shut up, can't you? And for God's sake stand still.' He was hard to get along with, most of the time. So I said, 'If you have to keep it so damn cold in here, how can a girl keep from shivering?' You see, I wasn't wearing anything."

Cook thought, irresistibly, of long bare legs. ("Regardless.") He said, "What did he seem to be fuming about, Miss Farmer?"

"When I thought he might be talking to me. Because it was clearer than the rest, and louder, of course, he said 'Best thing I've done for years. And a lot of Goddamn love seats.' I said 'What, mister?' and he told me to shut up."

Cook didn't get it, and said he didn't get it.

"A picture, of course, mister," Rachel said. "What else? Mostly he talked about pictures. But this time he sounded mad."

"At somebody?"

"I thought so. It sort of faded in and out. And of course, every now and then, he yelled at me to stand still, for God's sake. But they all do that. Anyway, I was cold. Once he said something that sounded like, 'Get away with it.' As if somebody wasn't going to. You know how people sound when they're mad?"

"Yes. Any idea what he meant by love seats?"

"He sounded as if he didn't like them. I don't myself, really. Not long enough, you know."

Tony Cook was a little afraid he did know.

"You thought he was angry about something?" Cook said, letting the shortness of love seats lie. "Or at somebody? More than he usually was? More–" he sought the word–"grumpy? As if something had come up that annoyed him?"

"Of course, mister. Why did you think I called you? Not that I didn't enjoy last evening. I don't say I didn't."

"So did I," Cook said.

"I haven't anything really on tonight," she said. "That is, I have, but it's nothing I can't get out of. And it would mean going uptown. To one of those chichi places. It always does with him."

She was, Cook thought, one hell of a witness. He was surprised by the irritation with her which crept in under the thought–by the degree of the irritation.

"Mad at somebody," he said. "The best thing he'd done for years. Love seats. And somebody not getting away with something."

"You don't listen very well, do you, mister? Of course, he kept rubbing his face. That may have annoyed him, I guess. Made him grumpy."

"Rubbing?"

"As if it itched," she said. "Don't beards itch when you shave them off? I mean where they were? The one he shaved off after he popped back from Spain."

"I never wore a beard," Cook heard himself say. "Will you be home this afternoon, Miss Farmer?"

"On official business?"

"For a telephone call. About going to a place that isn't chichi."

"Around three, I think," Rachel Farmer said. "He'll be grumpy, probably. But that doesn't really matter, does it?"

Cook felt rather grumpy himself as he took a subway uptown to Thirty-third Street. Mostly he was grumpy because he felt that Rachel Farmer had been on the verge of saying something coherent. But a little he was grumpy because he wondered who the hell was the "him" she talked about. Not that it was any of his business. His business was in stores which contained art galleries.

The street floor of the first store he went to was crowded. Most of those hurrying through it, or loitering through it, or standing with impatience at counters, were women. Here and there was a docile man who gave the impression of clinging in bewilderment to apron strings. There was an information desk and Cook waited at it, feeling docile and bewildered. When it was his turn he got, "Furniture, Seventh Floor. Elevators in the rear." He went to the rear; he went up, jostled in the car by women. (And one docile man.) He emerged into acres of furniture. Signs said: "Sleep Shop," "Living Room, Contemporary," "Living Room, Traditional," "For Outdoor Living." No sign said "Art Gallery." Cook wandered for a time among sofas and deeply upholstered chairs. He found a clerk and found his way.

The art gallery was in a distant corner, as if tucked there by afterthought. There was nobody in it, at first. Cook looked at pictures on the walls. They made a good deal more sense than the ones he had seen in Shackleford Jones's studio. You could tell what they were about, for the most part. One picture, which Cook rather liked, was about a horse in a pasture. He could tell with no difficulty at all that it was about a horse.

A spruce young man came to him and said, "Can I help you, sir?" without any conviction in his voice.

Cook wanted to see whoever was in charge; whoever was head of the department. That would be Mr. Bingham. Mr. Bingham, unfortunately, was in the executive offices, in conference. If there was something the spruce young man could do?

"Mr. Bingham," Cook said. "Police business." He said it like a policeman, and the spruce young man said, "Goodness!" He was afraid Mr. Bingham ––

Cook took his badge out of a pocket and held it toward the spruce young man. "I suppose," the spruce young man said, "I could try to reach Mr. Bingham on the ––"

A rather heavy and considerably older man came into the gallery room and the clerk said, "Here he is now," with relief in his voice, and then, "Mr. Bingham. This gen–a police officer would like to see you."

Bingham's broad face showed surprise and then, Cook thought, a hint of uneasiness. He beckoned and walked over to a desk in a corner of the room and sat behind it and motioned toward a chair, which Cook moved so that he faced the desk. Bingham, whose voice was appropriately heavy and a little husky, said, "How can I help you, officer?"

Cook told him how. At the mention of Jones's name, Bingham made appropriate sounds of regret, using tongue and teeth, and producing something like "tchk." It was a great pity about Mr. Jones. There had been a real talent there. Not, of course, to everyone's taste.

The store had never bought any of Shackleford Jones's paintings. Not precisely the sort of paintings most customers would go for. "Our clientele wants the representational," he said, and looked at Cook with some doubt. Cook nodded his head. "For a hundred dollars, if possible," Bingham said. "Something quite understandable. Preferably in blue, for some reason. Although yellow is quite popular just now."

"You were never offered a painting by Mr. Jones?"

Now that was another matter. It was, come to think of it—Bingham paused for a moment, coming to think of it—an interesting coincidence. He looked at the ceiling.

"A month or two ago," he said. "In April, I think it was, a man telephoned me. Knew who I was, incidentally. Asked for me by name. Identified himself as Shackleford Jones. Of course, I knew the name. He wanted to know whether we would be interested in looking at some of his work. Said he had several small things which he would sell for quite reasonable prices. I asked him what he thought a reasonable price and he said that he would let one of them go for seven hundred and fifty."

Bingham had been reluctant, but he had said "No," and that he was sorry.

"A Shack Jones would have lent a cachet to the gallery," Bingham told Detective Cook. "But it wouldn't have sold. Not at the price we'd have had to ask. Probably not at any price, really. Modern art is for special tastes. I was, frankly, astonished that he would offer work to us. The Museum of Modern Art. Yes. Of course. They have at least one of his, I believe."

"You were puzzled that he offered you pictures?"

"Astonished, as I said. Puzzled—well, not entirely. I supposed he needed ready cash. Quick cash. To be honest with you, a good many painters do. Even men who are accepted. Who normally sell through established dealers."

"Did you happen to know Mr. Jones?"

"Only by reputation. If you mean, did I recognize his voice, no. But I had no reason to think that it was not Jones who called. He was—seemed to be—knowledgeable. Except, obviously, about the prices we could afford to pay, and make a profit."

Cook took a Sixth Avenue bus uptown and left it in the Fifties and walked to Fifth. He went to three stores on Fifth, and to two on Fifty-seventh and to one on Lexington.

Buyers for all of the galleries had been telephoned by a man who identified himself as Jones and offered to sell pictures. Four had not been interested. Two had considered and promised to call back. One of them, after consideration, had not called. One had, at the number he had been given. He had not been answered. He had checked in the Manhattan directory and found the number under, "Jones, Shackleford (bus.)." There was another listing, "Jones, Shackleford (res.)." One buyer had made an appointment to go to Jones's studio and look at the pictures offered.

"Hell of a time finding the place," a wiry man named Askew told Cook. "And a hell of a place when I did find it. And all my trouble for nothing."

It had been for nothing because, when he found the door to the studio, there was a sign on it. The sign read: "Go Away." He had knocked on the door and got no answer and had obeyed the sign's injunction.

This had been about a month before, Askew thought. First or second week in May.

The other galleries had been called, like Bingham, in April.

His doorbell-ringing took Tony Cook all the morning and a little of the afternoon. He went back to Twentieth Street and Shapiro was not there. He had probably gone to lunch. Cook went to the most likely nearby restaurant; the one most of them used. Shapiro was sitting at a corner table and looking, in the dimness of the room, as morose as usual. He was eating a hot roast beef sandwich and drinking beer. He motioned toward a chair and Cook sat in it and motioned toward the sandwich and said, "Any good?"

"No worse than usual," Shapiro told him.

A waiter came and Cook ordered a hot roast beef sandwich and a bottle of Michelob. The waiter said, "Nope. Sorry, sergeant." And, "Making out all right, captain?" to Shapiro. Promotions were quick in Jack's Chop House.

Cook said that Miller's High Life would be fine, and told Shapiro where the bell-ringing had got him. He also, after hesitating momentarily, told him of Rachel Farmer's telephone call.

"It was always a man who called the galleries," Shapiro said. "Presumably Jones himself. That's interesting, isn't it, Tony? Most of them in April, the most recent about a month ago. Remember what Mrs. Dedek told us?"

Anthony Cook remembered.

"Of course," Shapiro said, "people aren't always very exact about time. But it would make quite a spread, wouldn't it? Between three weeks and two months or thereabouts."

Cook swallowed hot roast beef sandwich and said, "It certainly would."

"Jones set great store by that beard of his, apparently," Shapiro said. "Thought everybody knew him by it. And apparently a good many people did. May have thought that with his beard shaved off nobody would recognize him."

Cook agreed there was that.

"Could be he was around a time before he let anybody know he was," Shapiro said, speaking primarily to his almost empty beer glass. "Disguised by the absence of a beard." He looked at Tony Cook and said, "Seem reasonable?"

"Not very," Cook said. "Because why?"

He was told that that was a good point.

"Called everybody but Bryant and Washburn, apparently," Shapiro said. "Wonder why he didn't call them, don't you, Tony?"

Cook sipped beer and said he did.

"All the art galleries you went to this morning," Shapiro said, "were connected with furniture departments? Adjuncts of the furniture departments?"

"Yes."

"That's the setup at Bryant and Washburn's, too," Shapiro said. "Have to walk between and around a lot of sofas and chairs to get to it."

"Same with all of them," Cook said.

"When we've finished lunch," Shapiro said, "you might make that call to Miss Farmer. She might get back earlier than she thought. You might ask her if she can fix the time Jones came back from Spain. Come closer to it than Mrs. Dedek seems to have. Oh—and if Jones ever said anything to her about a painting he called 'The Melting Clown.' When he was mumbling while he worked and she posed for him."

The portfolio of drawings was an awkward thing to lug. Dorian was somewhat annoyed with herself. She should have called the messenger service early, instead of spending the morning choosing the sketches—the impertinent drawings for institutional advertisements, the cartoons for magazines—which she wanted to show. When, with a dozen selected and put together in the portfolio, she had called the messenger service its response had been, in effect, "Huh?"

It was Saturday afternoon, the messenger service reminded her. It was a Saturday afternoon, moreover, in mid-June. Everything was pretty much closed up, including places which needed messenger service. And it was a day off for most of the messengers. They would, of course, do their best. Roy Expediters always did their best. But they couldn't really guarantee anything about time. If Mrs. Weigand had called earlier ——

"Forget it," Dorian told Roy Expediters and hung up and called the garage for the Buick. She lugged the portfolio down a corridor and into an elevator.

She waited on the sidewalk for the arrival of the Buick and waited for some minutes. (The garage also had mentioned that it was Saturday afternoon and that it was, resultingly, understaffed.) The doorman–not George; George was off on summer Saturdays–helped her lodge the portfolio in the Buick.

She drove across town and found the traffic sparse. One reason for this, it became evident in East Seventy-ninth Street, was that a large percentage of the city's cars were spending the day against the city's curbs. She found a place for the Buick a block from the Dedek Galleries, and wrestled the portfolio out of the car and lugged it back. She got it to the door of the Dedek Galleries and found the door locked.

She should, obviously, have telephoned first. But Myra Dedek had been firm about delivery of the drawings that day and had, by implication, left the whole of the day available. Dorian peered through the glass of the window. The main display room was lighted, but at first it seemed empty.

Then, a little dimly, she saw Weldon Williams walk into the room from the rear. He was not dressed to receive patrons; he wore slacks and what appeared to be a sweat shirt. Dorian tapped knuckles on the glass. Williams began to take a picture down from a wall, deep in the room. Dorian got a quarter from her coin purse and rapped with that. The edge of the quarter made a sharp, clear sound on the glass.

Williams heard the sound. He turned from the wall and faced the door and made a gesture with his right hand. The gesture was not of welcome, but of dismissal. Dorian rapped again with the coin and Williams shrugged his shoulders, a little overdoing it. He mouthed a word, and a little overdid that, too. But the word clearly was "Closed." Dorian rapped again. He turned back and lifted hands toward the picture he was taking from the wall, and Dorian, annoyed by then with everything, rapped sharply and continued to rap. Williams raised both hands in a gesture of hopelessness and turned from the distant wall and walked toward the door. When he reached it, he looked through the glass at Dorian and began to shake his head. But he stopped that after a single shake and reached for the doorknob.

He was sorry; they were closed–closed, in fact, for the summer. He was just tidying up; putting pictures in the vault. If he had known it was Mrs. Weigand . . .

She pointed toward the portfolio, which was propped against her hip.

"I know you're closing," she told Weldon Williams. "Mrs. Dedek wanted these before you did. For a show in September. So, take them and tell Mrs. Dedek —"

But he had moved by then. He picked up the portfolio and stepped around Dorian to let her go ahead of him into the gallery. She said, "There's no need for me to . . ." but by then she had gone into the big, cool room, and Weldon Williams had closed the door after them.

"I'm terribly sorry," he said. "After the trouble you must have gone to. So many things to do when we're closing up. She did say you were sending the sketches up. And how co-operative you were. And–it just went out of my mind. I can't tell you how sorry I —"

"It doesn't matter," Dorian said. "They're here now. Tell Mrs. Dedek —"

"She'll want to see you," Williams said. "And look at what you've brought us. I'm certain she will. If you'll just come along up."

He picked up the portfolio. It did not seem awkward for him to carry. Of course, he evidently lugged much heavier things–framed paintings among them–in the course of his duties at the gallery. He carried the portfolio toward the stairs which Dorian had climbed the day before.

She hesitated for a moment and looked around the room. It was impossible to be in a room of paintings without looking around it.

Now there was not much to see; two of the walls were bare of pictures. Those now, presumably, were in the air conditioning, and behind the locks, of the gallery vault. The one Williams had been taking down was one of three remaining on that wall.

It was a rather large painting–a painting of curving lines and softened colors. At first neither lines nor colors seemed more than design. Then, partially, elusively, they shaped themselves into something more. What was perhaps a man emerged from the canvas.

If a man, a dissolving one, outlines of face and body indistinct; a man, if a man, in slow collapse. A man, if a man, who wore a conical hat, like a dunce cap. The cap, if a cap, was dissolving, too. Was melting. *Melting*. That was the word. It was a word suddenly very clear in Dorian's mind.

"Are you coming, Mrs. Weigand?" Weldon Williams said, from the foot of the stairs.

For a moment, Dorian continued to look at the picture. She could not make out the signature from where she stood. But she was almost certain that the signature, if she could make it out, would confirm what she already was quite sure of. She would tell Nathan Shapiro how sure she was.

Dorian joined Weldon Williams at the foot of the staircase. She walked up it ahead of him.

XV

THERE WAS NO place to park in the Seventy-ninth Street block. Cook wheeled the police car slowly through it and waited for lights to change and rolled on into the next block. They were lucky near the end of it; a car pulled out ahead and left a space against the curb. Cook backed the car into it. It was too close to a fire hydrant, as the car which had left a vacancy had been. That couldn't be helped. They walked back the way they had come.

They were almost at the avenue when Shapiro said, "Wait a minute, Tony," and walked back several cars and leaned down between two of them so he could see the license number on a Buick. It had been a hunch; the car was one of many thousands of Buicks of the same model and color. But it was a good hunch. They walked on until they came to the white four-story building which, with the utmost discretion, admitted to being the Dedek Galleries. A station wagon was parked in front of it.

Shapiro tried the knob of the reticent green door and nothing came of that. They looked through the glass of the door and looked into a large, lighted room. It was empty. Most of the walls were bare. Shapiro looked for a bell push and found none and knocked on the door and that, too, came to nothing.

"Could be we're late," Cook said and Shapiro sighed, thinking that all too probable, and knocked again. He knocked several times again, each time more loudly. Cook leaned down and examined the doorknob, which had a keyhole in it. He said, "I've got the gimmick. Want I should?"

"Not yet," Shapiro said, and knocked again on the glass of the small green door.

Mrs. Myra Dedek appeared from somewhere in the rear of the room and walked across it briskly, and Shapiro knocked again on the door, using a key against the glass. He got a fine sharp sound but no response to it, although he thought that Mrs. Dedek turned her head a little as if she looked toward the door. But if she did she apparently saw no one beyond it. She walked, still briskly, to a flight of stairs at one side of the room and up the stairs.

"Maybe she's deaf," Cook said, and Shapiro said, "Could be," and knocked again. Using the gimmick was the last resort; using gimmicks to open locked doors is no more legal for policemen than for anybody else. It makes a bad impression. Shapiro tapped with his key, almost hard enough to break the glass. Which would not have been legal, either. After several minutes, something did come of this. Weldon Williams came of it–came down the stairs Myra Dedek had gone up. He came to the door and stood on the other side of it and caressed his beard. Then he shook his head. Then, leaning close enough to the door so that his voice carried through it, he said, "Closed for the summer."

Williams had a poor memory for faces, Shapiro thought. Maybe he was shortsighted. Shapiro took his badge out of a pocket and held it against the glass. He reinforced the suggestion with the word, "Police," spoken loudly. Williams removed his right hand from his beard to the doorknob and turned and the snap lock clicked. He opened the door.

He seemed surprised to see Shapiro and Cook. He said, "Lieutenant somebody, isn't it? We're closed for . . ."

But then he shrugged, and Shapiro and Cook followed him into the lighted, empty room.

"Mrs. Weigand here?" Shapiro said.

Williams looked surprised again and shook his head.

"Arranged to meet her," Shapiro said. "Probably she'll be along. Mrs. Dedek here?"

"Upstairs," Williams said. "But —"

"I'd like a few words with her," Shapiro said. "Point or two to clear up. About her finding —"

He stopped because Myra Dedek was coming down the stairs. When she was at the bottom of them she said, "I told you I heard somebody," and said that to Weldon Williams, with reproach. Then, to Shapiro, she said, "There are so many things to do when we're closing for the season," and, after a momentary pause, added, "Lieutenant." She paused again and said, "I suppose some more questions. I hope it won't take too long."

"It shouldn't," Shapiro said. He looked around the room. There were several benches on which, presumably, prospective customers could sit and consider paintings. There were also a few chairs. He said, "Rather expected to find Mrs. Weigand here, Mrs. Dedek."

"Did you?" Myra Dedek said. "She was here. Brought in some sketches for a show. But she left an hour ago, didn't she, Weldon?"

"More than that, I'd think," Williams said. "Just popped in and dropped her portfolio and popped out again. Didn't say anything about expecting you, Lieutenant. Or Mr. —" He looked at Anthony Cook, who helped him by saying, "Cook."

Williams stroked his beard and looked at Myra, rather as if awaiting instruction.

"I'm sure you can get on with what you're doing, Weldon," she said, and then turned to Shapiro and said, "Can't he?"

"Rather he didn't," Shapiro said. "Why don't the two of you sit down some place? Unless your office, Mrs. Dedek?"

Her office was a "terrible mess." He had said it shouldn't take long. But . . .

She said, "Come on, Weldon. Seems there's no help for it," and crossed the room to one of the benches. Williams followed her and they sat side by side. Shapiro pulled a chair in front of them and sat on it and saw, without appearing to see, that for a moment Williams's hand touched a hand of the woman beside him. A touch of reassurance?

Cook leaned against a wall and took his notebook out.

"If it's about that picture Dorian was so mixed up about," Myra Dedek said. "I suppose she told you about that mistake of hers? She's been quite persistent about it, Oscar Bracken tells me."

"The one that wasn't by Mr. Jones," Shapiro said. "No, not primarily about that, Mrs. Dedek. About your discovery of. . . ." He paused. "Come to that," he said. "Speaking of Mr. Bracken. You expect to get the job you asked him about, Mr. Williams?"

Williams repeated the word "job" with a rising inflection and apparent astonishment.

"Way I understand it," Shapiro said. "May have got it wrong." He sighed. "Often do," he said. "Job in the Bryant and Washburn art gallery for the summer, I understood you asked about. While this gallery is closed."

"Weldon," Myra said. "Did you really? With all the things you promised to help me with?"

Williams caressed his beard again. He seemed to Shapiro to be very fond of it.

"Just for a few hours a day, Mrs. Dedek," Williams said. "Still have plenty of time for other things. Anyway, I gather he hasn't anything open."

"I should hope not," Myra Dedek said. She looked intently at her assistant. (Who had patted her hand in reassurance?) "I'm really surprised, Weldon."

"Happened to be in the store," Williams said. "Went up to take a look at the gallery and ran into Oscar. Just a spur of the moment thing. Surprised old Oscar thought it worth mentioning to the police."

"Heard you were there," Shapiro said. "Wondered about it. We wonder about a lot of things. Get us nowhere for the most part. How did Mrs. Weigand's hands look, Mrs. Dedek?"

"Hands? Whatever . . . ?"

"Almost got run down by a bus outside the store," Shapiro said. "Banged her hands up a little. Apparently stumbled on the curb or something."

"Lieutenant," Myra Dedek said, and for the first time her tone was sharp, almost combative. "I told you we had a hundred things to do. Do you have to waste our time this way? If Dorian Weigand's hands bother you, whyn't you ask her?"

"Sorry," Shapiro said. "I realize I'm wandering. Apt to, they tell me. Nothing to do with you, I realize. Or Mr. Williams. Did happen about the time you were in the store, Mr. Williams. Or leaving it. Police cars. An ambulance. Thought you might have seen it."

"No. Can't say I did."

His hand did go back to his beard.

"She had a notion somebody pushed her," Shapiro said, and shook his head. "Given to notions apparently."

"She must be," Myra said. "This nonsense about the picture she thought Shack had done. Urban something or other, or something like —"

She stopped rather suddenly.

"'Cityscape,'" Shapiro said. "The title of Mr. Shayburn's painting. The title the store gave it, anyway. But I don't want to waste your time. What I came to ask you, will you tell me again about going to Mr. Jones's studio? Hate to bring back such an unpleasant experience, but there's a point I'm not too clear about."

"I told the detective —"

"I know you did. Have to go over and over things. As exactly as you can, Mrs. Dedek."

She couldn't see why the police didn't get things right the first time. However . . .

"He'd told me he had some new canvases he wanted me to look at. I happened to be down his way —"

"You didn't telephone him first? To be sure he'd be there? But, then, you had a key, didn't you? Didn't matter whether he was there or not. You could tell him your reactions to the new canvases that evening, if he wasn't at the studio."

"There was never any point in calling him," Myra Dedek said. "He didn't answer the telephone."

And then, for an instant, her eyes narrowed as she looked at the sad-faced lieutenant of detectives.

"What do you mean, 'that evening'?" she asked him.

"Probably got something mixed up," Shapiro said. "Afraid I do sometimes. You went to the studio and . . . ?"

"Knocked at the door. Used my key and opened the door a little and called his name. When he didn't answer I opened the door wider and saw —" She put her hands over her eyes for a moment. "Saw him lying there," she said. "And the gun on the floor. And the–the awful blood."

"Bad thing to walk in on," Shapiro said. "Hate to have to make you remember it, Mrs. Dedek. You didn't go into the room? To make sure he was dead?"

She said, "No," and then again, *"No!"* She said, "I knew he was dead. You could tell from–from the way he was lying. I think I screamed and then–then called for help. Down the stairs. And some man, after a long time, heard me and came. I told the first policemen all this. Why do you keep making me go over it?"

"Just to be sure I've got it straight," Shapiro told her. "You know a man named Briskie, Mrs. Dedek? Painter. Does murals, I understand."

She knew his work. Thought she had met him. And why on earth . . . ?

"He's told us an odd story," Shapiro said. "We get a lot of them. Not very believable, some of them. Mr. Briskie says he was at Jones's studio Thursday, Mrs. Dedek. Says he found Jones's body before you did. Had gone there to buy a painting, he says. Anyway, after he found Jones dead, he says he went looking for this picture. Not very likely, of course. You didn't see him there, obviously."

"There wasn't anybody there. There couldn't have been."

"Well," Shapiro said, "it's a big barn of a place. Lots of things a man could hide behind, if he had some reason to want to hide. And you didn't really go into the studio, did you? Didn't look around it for anything. Like, say, a list of paintings?"

She did not know what he was talking about. She had done only what she had just told him–stood at the door, and . . .

"According to Briskie's unlikely story," Shapiro said, "he was in the rear of the studio. Heard somebody knock at the door and then use a key. And call Jones's name from the doorway. Call it very loudly, he says. And then, while he was still behind something in the rear of the room, he says he heard someone walking around for–oh, for perhaps a minute. A woman's heel taps, he says."

"Not mine, if that's what you're getting at. As for the list —" She broke off.

Shapiro did nothing to indicate he had heard her last four words.

"Briskie," Shapiro said, "told me he looked around whatever he was behind and saw who was walking around the room. And –he says it was you, Mrs. Dedek. You'd gone back to the door by the time he saw you, according to this story of his. Were standing in the doorway, screaming. But he's quite certain that before you stood in the doorway and called for help you had walked over to Jones's body."

"He's lying. I–why would I go over to poor Shack's body? When I could see from the door ––" Suddenly she covered her face with her hands and her body shook. Weldon Williams put a sustaining hand on her shoulder. "All I could bear to see," Myra Dedek said, and took her shielding hands down from her face.

Then she stood up suddenly.

"So that's it," she said. "He was killed. And Maxwell Briskie killed him, didn't he? Because of that picture poor Shack did a long time ago of Max's wife. And was going to show until I talked him out of it. And–*of course!* You've known it all along, haven't you? He went back Thursday to see–to see that he hadn't slipped up–hadn't forgotten something which wouldn't fit in with suicide. That's it, isn't it?"

"Yes," Shapiro said. "I think that was very probably the reason for the Thursday visit, Mrs. Dedek. Murderers do get to worrying. Sometimes decide to tidy things up. Or be sure they are tidy. As for the list–what, Mrs. Dedek? I'm afraid I interrupted something you started to say."

But then he was himself interrupted. Somebody knocked on the glass of the street door. Both Myra Dedek and Weldon Williams started to get up, but Nathan Shapiro was ahead of them. He said, "Probably Mrs. Weigand," and took long strides to the door and opened it.

It was bright outside and Oscar Bracken's eyes apparently did not adjust immediately to the relatively dimmer light inside.

He said, "Here's the damn thing, and from now on you two can count me ––"

Then he looked at Shapiro and stopped.

"Out," Shapiro said, finishing the sentence for him.

Bracken had put the "damn thing" down on the floor so that

it leaned against the wall. It was a framed picture, wrapped in brown paper, tied up with cord.

Williams and Myra Dedek had crossed the room side by side and Myra spoke from a little distance.

"I didn't mean you had to bring it yourself, Oscar," Myra said. "Such a big, awkward thing. I could have sent a messenger over for it. It was merely because I wouldn't be here Monday that I couldn't wait for the parcel service. And I did want to get it into the vault for the summer. Weldon?"

"I'll take it down," Weldon Williams said and reached for the picture.

"Let's unwrap it first," Shapiro said. "I always like to unwrap presents."

He put a hand in his pocket, fingers searching for a knife to cut the heavy cord. And Weldon Williams grabbed the awkward parcel the painting made and ran with it.

"You fool!" Myra Dedek called to him, yelled after him. *"You impossible fool!"*

"Hold them, Tony," Shapiro said, not so loudly but loudly enough. "Mr. Bracken's going to want to talk."

He said the last as he ran after Williams, who moved fast for a man carrying an awkward parcel–who ran under a stairway. Then he ran downstairs to the basement before Shapiro caught up with him.

Williams stood in a wide corridor and had dropped the framed picture, which lay on the floor behind him.

He had a steel bar in his right hand and held it by the notched crook. A tool for wrenching open wooden crates, Shapiro thought, as Williams lifted the tool-turned-to-weapon and started toward him.

Shapiro had to shoot the steel rod out of Weldon Williams's hand, which was a little risky, since bullets ricochet in confined places. The rod jumped out of Williams's hand, and the hand dropped down with the shock of the blow.

The bar flew the length of the short corridor and clattered with violence against a metal door at the end of it.

"Open it," Shapiro told Williams, and kept his revolver pointed. Williams shook his stunned right hand and hesitated.

"Get going," Shapiro said and moved the revolver a little.

Williams got going.

He did not need a key to open the metal door of the gallery vault. It had a snap lock. There was no knob on the inner surface.

"It took you rather long," Dorian Weigand said, and walked out of the vault. "Not that it isn't nice and cool in there. Did you have to kill anyone, Lieutenant?"

Williams, with Shapiro's revolver directing him, carried the painting back up the stairs. He used his left hand and still shook his right, to shake feeling back into it.

Anthony Cook was holding Myra Dedek and Bracken by standing in front of the street door with his revolver dangling. When Shapiro came from behind the stairs Bracken shouted at him. "They can't drag me into anything. They can count me —"

He stopped again, and again, after a second, Shapiro finished for him. "Out," Shapiro said. "I heard you before, Bracken. Hold the picture up, Williams."

Williams held the big, flat parcel up and Shapiro cut the cords away and pulled the wrapping paper down.

It was just planes and colors to Nathan Shapiro. But then it seemed to be moving upward in its frame and he saw why somebody had called it "Cityscape." It didn't really look like a city. Still . . .

Dorian Weigand seemed to flow down to her knees in front of the painting which Williams held propped up on the floor. She peered at the lower right-hand corner of the picture.

"It's really quite a clear signature, once you know where Shack Jones hid it," Dorian said, and she turned to face Myra Dedek. "Not really anything that could be Shayburn, Myra," Dorian said.

Myra Dedek seemed not to hear. She sat rigid on a bench and looked with hard eyes at Weldon Williams.

"Fool," Myra said. "Fool. Fool. *Fool!*"

XVI

ANTHONY COOK WALKED from the subway station at West Fourth Street toward Gay Street. It was a little before seven–he had allowed himself plenty of time; subway service is diminished on Sundays–and the mid-June sun still was hot. He wore the gray summer suit which he usually wore on summer Sundays. The jacket was a little looser than he would have chosen if left to his own devices, but a gun shows under a jacket which fits too well. And Article 288 of the Rules and Regulations of the Police Department of the City of New York did not leave Detective Anthony Cook to his own devices.

"A member of the Force shall carry his service revolver at all times, except that a Colt or Smith & Wesson revolver, not less than a .32 calibre, may be carried under the following conditions:"

One of the conditions was that the member of the force be either a detective or off duty. Tony Cook was, at the moment, both. His .32 was a Smith & Wesson. It was not especially uncomfortable against his chest. He was used to its being there.

In the Gay Street vestibule he pressed the proper button and the answer was immediate and he climbed stairs and the door opened as he reached the top of them. For an instant he thought he must have pushed the wrong button.

She wore a white silk dress with a red belt around her slim waist and she wore stockings and high-heeled white shoes. The dress was sheer; she was wearing a slip under it. She was also wearing a bra.

She had done something to her black hair or, more probably, had had something done to it. It had been lank, falling straight almost to her shoulders. It was a little shorter now, and now it was softly waved. He looked down at her; although a tall man, he did not have to look far down. He said, "Well!" which was the first word to come into his mind.

She grinned at him. He had not especially noticed her mouth before. It was rather wide and became her well. It was also delicately contoured.

"Thanks, mister," Rachel Farmer said. "I hoped you would. All yesterday afternoon it took me, after you signed off. The door's open, mister. You can gawk inside."

Inside she sat on a sofa with her knees together. She said, "You bang the third panel to get it. Mine's sherry, you know. And there's bourbon and some gin I think, but I forgot the vermouth. The ice is in the bucket."

The ice was in the bucket and the bourbon was Old Fitzgerald, a hundred proof, and the sherry was La Ina, and, after he had poured drinks and sat down beside Rachel Farmer, Cook still felt that he was somehow in the wrong place. Not that it wasn't a fine place.

He looked at the girl and said, "Well!" which was the word which still came into his mind.

"All right, mister," Rachel said. "Haven't you been surprised enough for now?"

And she raised her wine glass to clink with his heavier glass. He had not noticed before how delicate her hands were. Her nail polish did not match, but blended with, the off-red of her belt.

He said he was sorry about last night, but that it couldn't be helped and that probably he didn't need to tell her that, since it had been in the papers. Cook's own name had been included in the account in the *Times* but that was nothing to mention boastfully.

TWO FACE HOMICIDE CHARGES IN PAINTER'S DEATH, the headline had read, and, in a bank: "Third Held as Material Witness."

"Headlines," Rachel said. "I don't really read the newspapers very much, mister. Especially the Sunday ones, when they're so big. Advertisements of dresses sometimes and about the poor dear Mets."

"Myra Dedek and that assistant of hers," Cook said. "It looks as if they killed Shackleford Jones. Anyway, that she did and he helped. And that a man named Bracken, who's head of the art gallery at Bryant and Washburn's, was in on it–anyway, on what led up to it. And —"

"I read that far," Rachel said. "Then it was continued somewhere and I found it but it was right next to a robe I liked. Only, you can't tell much from these sketches they use nowadays, can you?"

"I guess you can't," Tony Cook, who had no idea one way or another, told the unexpected girl who sat beside him on the sofa.

"Tony," she said, "you're sort of a dear. I did read most of the rest of it; only I thought, He's one of the arresting officers and he's taking me to dinner tonight, unless somebody else kills somebody and he has to break the date, and he's the one who worked it out, probably, and I'll get him to tell me. Because the newspapers are all full of 'alleges.' Do you know a poem by Robert Graves about cats?"

"Sort of nuts," he had told the lieutenant. And one hell of a witness, he had told himself. And, of course, a dame who was quite a dame.

"No," Detective Anthony Cook said to Miss Rachel Farmer, speaking as quietly as possible.

"'Cats make their points by walking round them,'" she said. "Newspapers are like that. Only it's 'alleging around them,' isn't it? Why would Myra Dedek want to kill poor Shack? Not that I ever liked what I knew of her."

"For money," Cook said. "She had got herself out on a financial limb with the gallery. She thought he was away for a year and that she could sell off some of his paintings and keep the money. Still can't get used to the idea myself–that pictures like that are really worth money."

"Yes, Tony," Rachel Farmer said. "Sometimes they are worth quite a lot of money. Haven't you heard about the cultural explosion? It's all over everywhere. And compared to a lot of them Shack was pretty–coherent. If you'd said that to him he'd really have shot himself, I guess. Or you. But it's safe to say it now he's dead. Go on, mister."

He looked at her again.

"Go on, Tony," Rachel Farmer said. "And then we'll have another drink and go to Charles'. Because I've got a new dress and you think it's pretty. And because it costs more than the lasagna place, we'll go Dutch and . . ."

Tony Cook took time out to resent that suggestion. Then did go on with it; went on with what they knew of it, and what they put together about it. "It was Shapiro worked it out," Cook said.

It remained speculative, he told her, and the lieutenant was uneasy about that. "He seems to be uneasy most of the time." Myra Dedek and Weldon Williams were, as was to be expected, doing nothing to help. Oscar Bracken, however, was doing his best to talk his way out of involvement–certainly out of involvement in murder. To that extent, he might succeed. He was, meanwhile, helping them to piece together a scheme which had started as theft and led on to murder. Because Myra Dedek needed money.

That they could prove, without too much difficulty. She had mortgage payments due–overdue–on the building she had bought to house the gallery. She did not have the money to meet the payments. The mortgage company had been growing increasingly insistent. Things like that could be proved.

She needed money, and there was the potential of money in Shackleford Jones's studio. She had a key to the studio, and Jones was in Spain and expected to remain there for a year or more. That Mrs. Dedek herself had told them. Enlist Williams as an accomplice; take the pictures most likely to sell and let them dribble onto the market.

"He would have come back sometime," Rachel said. "He'd have found out sometime."

"That paintings were missing? Yes. But if he'd stayed away as long as Mrs. Dedek thought he would they could have cashed in on a good many of the paintings and–the lieutenant thinks–spread the rest out thin. All over the country maybe."

They had started to do that, apparently. Williams had been crating pictures the day before; he had loaded some of them into a station wagon. They were going to get them out of the gallery. Planning to start selling them in the fall. Which they could then do safely, because, with Jones dead, Myra Dedek had an agreement which would permit her to sell openly.

He told Rachel about the agreement.

"What I think is," she said, "she planned all along to kill him. It would have made things so much simpler."

That might well be true. It would be difficult to prove.

Certain things they could prove. They could prove that someone representing himself as Jones, probably Williams, had offered to sell pictures to store galleries at a time when Jones was not in the country. And they had Oscar Bracken, who actually had bought one for Bryant & Washburn. As, wriggling now to get as far as he could out of bad trouble, he would willingly, even eagerly, testify.

"He was getting a cut?"

Not according to his story. But Myra Dedek had a hold on him and was ready enough to twist. Something to do with his authenticating fake paintings when he had his own gallery. It was to avoid exposure that he had bought the painting called "Urban Rectangles," or "Cityscape." He would admit he had bought it from Williams, just before Jones's unexpected return. He would testify that, when she heard that Jones was early back from Spain, Myra Dedek had telephoned him and instructed him not to hang the painting for sale.

He had agreed. But he had not been able to do what he promised.

"Seems," Cook said, "the head of the whole department—furniture floor—is interested in paintings. Poked around, Bracken says, and found the Shack painting and told Bracken to get the hell on with selling it. So Bracken had to hang it. And, what we're pretty sure happened, Jones saw it."

Probably—and here they were piecing mere probabilities together—by accident. One of the things they had found in Jones's papers was a bill from Bryant & Washburn for a sports jacket, purchased three weeks before. Apparently soon after he got back. While he was in the store he had, almost certainly, decided to visit the art gallery. He had found one of his own paintings there.

"Somebody would have recognized him," Rachel said. "With that beard of his."

"He'd gone to a barber and had the beard shaved off," Cook told her. "The day before he bought the sports jacket, according to the barber. Anyway, as well as he can remember."

"Tony," she said, "did you go around and ask all the barbers in the city if they shaved Shack Jones?"

"Not personally," he said. "There are fifty or so men working on it now. And a couple of policewomen. Now that we've gone out on a limb. One of the boys, with a before and after picture of Jones—before and after shaving, I mean—found a barber last night. And somebody else found the clerk who sold the sports jacket. Says, sure he sold a sports jacket that day, because his number's on the salescheck, but he can't remember when he sold a jacket to a man with a beard. Can't remember he ever did. Says, 'We don't get many beards here.'"

Jones had gone over the paintings in his studio and found thirty-two of them missing and had made a list of the missing ones. That they could prove; they had the typed list and a carbon of the list. They had found both in the vault of the Dedek Galleries, along with most of the paintings themselves, some crated, others waiting to be crated. Williams had been using the list as a check-off guide.

"One of the ones not crated," Cook told Rachel, sipping from his drink and trying to keep his mind on his subject, "was something Jones called 'The Melting Clown.' Doesn't make any sense to me, but most of them don't."

That one had still been on a gallery wall when Dorian Weigand took her sketches in—the sketches which had, she assumed and the police assumed, served Myra as an excuse to bring up the subject of the painting called "Cityscape" and deny it was by Jones. Dorian Weigand had seen "The Melting Clown" and jumped to an accurate conclusion.

"The lieutenant had asked her about it," Cook said. "She knew it fitted in some place. Williams saw her looking hard at it and realized she had recognized it. So, when the lieutenant and I showed up, he shut her in the vault to keep her from telling us about the clown picture."

"It was a silly thing to do," Rachel said. "Unless they were going to kill her."

It was, unless they were. Possibly Williams hadn't thought that far ahead. Quite possibly, as Myra Dedek had kept saying, he was a fool. Certainly, things had got beyond him—got beyond both of them. They were improvising, by then.

"Shack made a list," Rachel said. "Suppose you make us a drink?"

He poured sherry and bourbon.

"You've found the list," she said, and prompted. She also looked at her watch.

"Typed," Cook said, "on the portable in Jones's apartment. That we can prove. He sent a carbon to his wife. Presumably for safekeeping. He may, with or without the list, have gone to other store galleries, doing his own detective work. We don't know and probably won't know."

Several days after he had seen "Cityscape" at Bryant & Washburn, Jones had called Bracken and asked where he had got it. Bracken would testify to that. Bracken had a hide to save.

"He told Jones, he says, that Williams sold him the picture. He says he had, then, no idea Williams didn't have the right to sell it, since the Dedek Galleries was Jones's dealer. That may be true. It's what he'll say. He did call Mrs. Dedek and told her about Jones's question. And she told him to take the picture down. He says he began to wonder then, but he took it down."

"Only," Rachel said, "Mrs. Weigand saw it."

It was possible, Cook said, to be a little sorry for Bracken. What with one thing and another, he was kept hopping around like a flea. The head of the department found the picture missing and no record of its sale, and jumped Bracken about it. Bracken made some excuse—about its needing cleaning, he said. The excuse didn't satisfy the department head, who told Bracken to put it up again. Bracken did.

"He kept hoping somebody would buy the damn thing," Cook said. "But nobody did. Then Dorian Weigand, whom Bracken knew by sight, began to ask him about 'Cityscape.' He says he began to think something fishy was going on and called Mrs. Dedek again. She told him–he says–that there wasn't anything fishy. Only a little confusion which she would straighten out with Jones. Meanwhile, Bracken was to take the picture down again and send it back to her, and that she'd refund the money the store had paid for it. Bracken says he was pretty sure something was fishy, but he took the picture down."

Cook took a long swallow from his glass and looked at his own watch.

"We'll have to lean pretty heavily on Bracken," he said. "Anyway, the D.A.'s office will. It's not too happy. But, then, it never is, much. Bracken and odds and ends. Some of which we're looking for. We've pretty much got Williams cold on the slugging of Mrs. Jones to get the carbon, on account of he had the carbon. And how else would he have got it?"

"How did he know she'd be at the studio?"

"Jeremiah Osgood says he made the date with Mrs. Jones when she caught up with him in an elevator at Bryant and Washburn's. And that Williams was in the elevator and could have overheard. We suspect he acted on his own on that. As when he pushed Mrs. Weigand in front of a bus. If he did."

"Not when he killed poor Shack?"

Anthony Cook put his glass down rather hard on a table and said, "My dear girl. He didn't kill Jones. Myra did that. Got to thinking things over and decided it would be simpler to kill Jones than to explain to him. Also, with him dead she'd have a legitimate claim to the pictures she had already stolen. And Osgood and Mrs. Weigand agree that the pictures probably will be worth more with Jones dead than with Jones alive."

"Can you prove she killed him?"

They could, he thought, make it appear pretty damn likely. Briskie would help with that although they might have to put the screws on Briskie, who wouldn't be enthusiastic about explaining his presence in the studio on Thursday. But who would, Shapiro was pretty certain–told Cook he was pretty certain–testify that Myra Dedek had not stopped at the door that day, but had walked into the studio and over to the body, to be sure she had got the "suicide" straight the day before. Which wouldn't jibe with Myra Dedek's account, which was on record.

"I don't," Rachel said, "think that either Myra or Williams was very bright."

"Murderers aren't," Cook told her. "Anyway, the ones we catch. Shapiro says —"

He stopped, because Rachel Farmer had put her empty glass down on a table and was looking thoughtfully across the room at, he thought, nothing in particular.

"Looking for missing pieces?" Cook asked her.

She shook her head. But then she said, "Maybe I was, in a sort of way. I was thinking about squabs. Anyway, I was deciding whether I was hungry and squabs came into it. Not that I especially like squabs."

He sorted things out. It seemed to be becoming easier. He said, "You mean the ones Jones was going to feed to somebody? The ones the lieutenant found in the refrigerator? That convinced him Jones hadn't planned to kill himself?"

"Was it Dotty? She does like squabs. Only, I've always thought she liked Maxie a good deal. A lot, maybe."

"Probably we'll never know," he said. "Anybody."

He shrugged his shoulders. Again he said, "Anybody . . ." and let it hang.

She looked at him then. Then she said, "No, Tony. Not anybody." She stood up. He stood too, facing her.

"I've decided I am hungry," she said. "So —" She did not finish that, but looked at him. He did not move, but only looked back at her.

"No, Tony," Rachel said. "Don't muss my pretty dress." Then, suddenly, she grinned. "Now," Rachel Farmer added.